Deadly Don's Arranged Vows

An Age Gap Mafia Romance

Piper Raven

Copyright © 2024 by Piper Raven

All rights reserved.

No portion of this book may be reproduced in any form without written permission from the publisher or author, except as permitted by U.S. copyright law.

Contents

1. Carlo — 1
2. Isabella — 9
3. Carlo — 17
4. Isabella — 24
5. Carlo — 32
6. Isabella — 40
7. Carlo — 48
8. Isabella — 55
9. Carlo — 64
10. Isabella — 71
11. Carlo — 78
12. Isabella — 85
13. Carlo — 92
14. Isabella — 99
15. Carlo — 106

16.	Isabella	114
17.	Carlo	121
18.	Isabella	125
19.	Carlo	132
20.	Isabella	140
Deadly Don's Secret Baby Sneak Peek		150

Chapter 1

Carlo

And there she is . . .

My shoes click, capturing her attention as I walk over the marble ballroom floor. The moment her blue eyes meet mine, a smile breaks over her gorgeous face. "Oh, you must be the groom!" Stepping over a bundle of ribbons lying on the floor, she can't take her eyes off me. "Carlo Vietti, right?"

With a snap of my fingers, all others in the room vanish, leaving us alone. "And you are Isabella Conti, my best friend John's little sister."

Closing the distance between us, she holds out her hand. "I can't thank you enough for allowing me to put your wedding together."

The electricity bouncing back and forth between us as I shake her hand is undeniable. "I'm glad you could find some time for me, Isabella. John tells me you're trying to make a name for yourself as a wedding planner."

"I recently helped a friend of mine with her wedding, and it's become an obsession." She scans the room as if looking for someone. "And where is the lovely bride-to-be?"

"She's not in town." Offering her my arm, I like that she readily slips her hand into the crook of my elbow and follows me without hesitation. "I'm sure your brother has already told you the specifics of this thing."

As she's about half a foot shorter than I am, she looks up at me and gives me a slight nod. "He said you want me to do whatever I want."

Her golden hair falls in soft waves all the way down her back, and a light smattering of freckles peppers the bridge of her turned-up nose. I find I like the way she looks very much. "Yes, whatever *you* want."

She tugs me to a stop. "A wedding isn't about what someone else wants. It's about what the bride wants. The groom too—to some extent. But it's *never* what the wedding planner wants. Not ever."

I bet she's not even aware of how beautiful she is. Long legs, large breasts, and those blue pools that stare right into my soul. "Well, this wedding is going to be whatever the wedding planner wants. We're busy people, Isabella. Surely, you can understand that."

"Too busy to plan the biggest day of your lives?" Incredulous, she takes a step back, breaking our physical contact. "Wow. I can't wait to meet this woman who wants *nothing* to do with her own wedding. Will I meet her before the big day?"

I love her tenacity. "Probably not."

"Probably not," she mumbles to herself before turning her attention back to me. "Well, I'll make sure she's stunned when she sees what I've cooked up for the two of you." Moving toward me, she loops her arm through mine again. "So, where are you taking me, Carlo?"

"To the wine cellar. I thought we could pick out the wine for the wedding." It's only fitting that she helps choose the wine so that it can match the rest of the style she's envisioned for the wedding.

"Does your fiancé like white or red?" I feel every move she makes, even the slight shifting of her fingers, which mystifies me. I don't often connect to people this way.

"What do *you* prefer?" It should be something she likes.

Shaking her head, she laughs, a sound that makes me smile. "This is just so odd. I suppose I'll get used to it."

The door to the wine cellar is large and ornate, something I had brought in from a castle that fell in such disrepair that it had to be torn down. "Here we are." I watch her eyes, which grow large as she takes in the ancient door.

Placing her hand on the wood, she sighs. "I have only seen things this majestic in magazines." Her eyes glisten with delight. "This resembles pear wood, and it seems to be from the medieval period. I would think something of this grandeur would have been found in the home of an aristocrat living in Europe."

I adore a smart woman. "It's from a castle in Sicily. I must tell you that I find it fascinating that you knew that. Did you study ancient architecture in college?"

"I spent a summer in Italy, roaming the countryside and touring castles with my mother." Watery eyes tell me how much she misses her mother. "It was a trip for my eighteenth birthday.

Our last one together before she . . ." Unable to finish her thought, she closes her eyes while placing her hand on her chest.

I know all about the passing of her parents. Or at least what she's been told. John never told me how much she misses them. Her pain is obvious. I can actually feel the sad emotions that fill her, and all I can think about is getting rid of them.

"As your brother's best friend, I know what happened, Isabella." Running my hand over her shoulders, I want nothing more than to bring comfort to her.

Inhaling deeply, she pulls herself together with a speed that amazes me. "You keep referring to John as my brother. We're close and always have been, but I have never referred to him as my brother. He's my stepbrother. His father was my stepfather, and then he became my adoptive father. My mother is the only real family I had. And now she's gone." Her eyes close again as emotions threaten to pull her back under. But then she blinks a few times before smiling. "So, what's behind this door?"

"Wine. Lots and lots of wine." I open the door, and the lights on the staircase illuminate automatically. "Just down this staircase that came from the same castle the door did, you will find only the very best of wines."

Running one hand along the stone wall, she moves slowly down the stairs, holding my arm with her other hand to steady herself. "Your wife is sure to enjoy this feature of your home, Carlo."

"I hope she enjoys all the features of this home—there are many. I should show you around." She should see the whole mansion anyway.

"I would adore that," she says, gushing, all smiles as we head down to the cellar. When the lights sense us and come on, lighting up the entire area, she gasps. "Oh my!"

"It's spectacular, isn't it?" I never tire of seeing the marvels that the cellar holds.

Scanning the large room, she finally looks up at me. "You have an amazing home, Carlo."

The blue pools in her eyes shine as she smiles widely. I could look at her gorgeous face forever, but now is not the time to get lost in the woman. "So, let's find the wine we'll drink."

"Yes, let's find the perfect bottle for you to share with your wife. It should be as perfect as the marriage will be. This is a great cornerstone to build the rest of the wedding around. It will be a grand wedding that both of you will remember fondly forever. I promise you only great things will come from this wedding."

"I believe you, Isabella." Briefly, I cradle her face and gaze at her delicate features, then pull my hand away before it can get weird. "You were made for this type of work."

Her hand moves to her heart, and she glows with pride. "Thank you, Carlo. You have no idea how much that means to me. I want to be the best wedding planner in New York, which is a huge deal. Doing this wedding is setting me up for so much more. I can't thank you enough."

"It's me who should be thanking you. You've made things so easy for us." Moving us further along into the cellar, I gesture to the red wine section. "I'm sure you'll find something here in this area."

She kneels in front of the lower rack and begins searching the labels for what she wants. "So, where are you two going to honeymoon?"

"Wherever she wants." I don't care where we go. I don't care if we stay home. All I care about is getting married and beginning to make the family my legacy requires.

"Has she given you any ideas about where she might want to go?" Pulling out a bottle, she sets it to the side and then goes back to search for the perfect bottle.

"None." Leaning back against the wall, I pull my cell from my pocket to check my emails while I'm waiting.

"You sound a bit disinterested in the honeymoon, Carlo."

I look down to find her scowling at me, and it makes me laugh. "By the look on your face, I can see that you feel the honeymoon is very important."

"And you don't?" She clasps her hands together as if praying.

"I'm sure we can figure out where we want to go—if we want to go anywhere. This is a lovely home, after all. I have everything we need right here. A spa with world-class masseuses. A theater where we can be entertained by movies that haven't even been seen in theaters yet. I can get any cast of any Broadway production to perform right here if I want." Turning my attention back to my emails, I see some I have to respond to.

Rising, she checks out wine bottles on higher racks and becomes silent. It shouldn't bother me, but somehow it does. I feel a little like she's disappointed in me over the lack of honeymoon plans, which is silly and, quite frankly, none of her business.

Going back to my response to my cousin's email, I let him know I'll be sending him a truckload of cigars and cigarettes for his casinos. "You like to gamble?" I ask, just to start her talking again.

"Not really." She runs her hands through her hair, then pushes it back, away from her face. "Why do you ask?"

"My cousin, Giovanni, has casinos. I thought you might like to check one out sometime." I'm focused on tapping in some instructions about something I need my cousin to get for me, and then I notice her staring at me with wide eyes, her mouth agape. "What?"

"I hope I'm reading this wrong, but it kind of sounds like you'd like me to go with you to a casino."

"And what if I would like that?"

"Um, so much is wrong with that, Carlo. You're about to be a married man. You're engaged."

Fuck! Oh yeah, I'm getting married.

I can't let her know I was actually asking her out. "I didn't mean it like that. It's just that I have a stake in my cousin's business, and sending new customers his way is a thing I do. You shouldn't take the things I say out of context. I'm about to be a married man, as you pointed out."

Her cheeks begin to glow red with embarrassment. Even flushed cheeks look good on her. "Sorry. I feel foolish now."

"Don't. I have this way about me that makes women think I want them when I don't. That's all. It's a gift and a curse."

"Especially now that you're getting married." With a short nod, she seems to be back to her sweet self. "Anyway, you're a wealthy man who's obviously well-traveled and a bit on the exotic side. You kind of exude sexuality and power. You're the epitome of an Italian stallion."

Of all the things I have been called, that's not one of them. "If you say so, Isabella. Want to know my take on you?"

Looking up at the ceiling, she shakes her head. "I know I might come off as confident, but I'm pretty insecure. I don't know if I can take anything negative."

"Nothing I would ever say about you would be negative. I happen to find you fascinating. So smart for a young woman. And put together like a classic feminine woman too."

Any man would be lucky to call her his wife. Not that just any man will get to do that.

Chapter 2

Isabella

Setting the table, I can't seem to wipe the smile off my lips. Not only am I working on the wedding of my dreams, but I'm also making a killing doing it. Plus, hanging out with Carlo was kind of spectacular.

The sound of dress shoes clicking against the tile floor prompts me to turn to see who is coming. "So, how was it today?" my stepbrother asks as he enters the dining room.

I try not to gush but fail miserably. "It was great! So much fun! And the mansion is gorgeous. I can't believe you got me the job of my dreams." He's already taken a seat at the small table, so I lean over his shoulder to kiss his bearded cheek. "Thank you so much!"

Grabbing my arms, he pulls me down and then kisses my cheek. "You are very welcome. I love seeing you happy."

John has always wanted me to be happy. He tried everything he could to make me laugh when I was a kid. I can't imagine my life without him in it.

Going to the kitchen, I come back with the roast beef, complete with baby carrots and sliced potatoes. "I made a roast after I got home today."

We'd made a habit of eating dinner together. When our parents were alive, it was a mandatory thing Mom made us do. After their deaths, John and I kept it up. It felt like a little bit of normalcy in a world that had been turned upside down.

"It smells and looks delicious. Tomorrow, I'll bring something home so you won't have to cook." John fills his plate. He's always been a voracious eater. "Did you get to meet Carlo?"

I nod, trying not to let my attraction for his best friend show on my face. "Yes. He's all man, isn't he?"

With a half grin, he nods. "I suppose he is. The man has his hands in all sorts of business dealings. He was born into money, but he's made his own money too. He's confident in every way imaginable. I guess you ladies would see him as all man."

"I know I shouldn't even think of him like that. He's not only about to get married, but he's my boss or client or whatever you call the person who pays you for work you do."

He nods before stabbing a forkful of roast and shoving it into his mouth. Picking up the glass of red wine I brought home from Carlo's cellar, he takes a large gulp to wash down the food. "Oh yeah, this is some of the good stuff. He let you bring some wine home, then?"

I find it odd that he can immediately tell the wine is from Carlo's collection. "How'd you know?"

"He and I have been best friends forever. I know my best friend's wine when I taste it. How much did he give you?"

"A case of red and a case of white, and then another case of burgundy because I mentioned that I enjoy a glass of that every now and then. He's very generous." As I sip the wine, I can't stop smiling as I think about how well Carlo's suit fit him. "He works out a lot, huh?"

"You lookin' at that man's body?" Winking at me, he nods. "Yeah, he works out like a demon." Patting his round stomach, he laughs. "That is something I do as little of as I can. But Carlo loves the gym. He's got one at his place. When you get right down to it, he's got everything at his place. I wonder why he ever goes anywhere with all he's got right under his very large roof."

"Did you know that he doesn't have a plan for their honeymoon?" I still can't wrap my head around that fact. "And what about his fiancée? Who is she? Where's she from? And is she someone who deserves a man like him?"

His dark brows raise as he smirks at me. "You sound a little jealous, Bella."

"I'm just asking about the woman I'm designing a wedding for," I say, crossing my arms over my chest. "Like, why doesn't she want anything to do with planning her wedding? What kind of woman cares nothing about her own wedding? I have to wonder if I'll even like her."

"Not that you need to." He shakes his head and then stabs more meat with his fork. "Where do you think a good honeymoon destination would be?"

"Oh, I don't know. It all depends on what the couple has in common. What they like. What they hate. It should be all about them—not that Carlo wants anything to be about them. It's weird, to be honest."

"Just do what he says, and things will go fine." After gulping the remainder of the wine from his glass, he grabs the bottle to refill it.

Nibbling on a carrot, I can't stop thinking about the bride and if she's really the right woman for a man like Carlo Vietti. "I know he's way older than I am, but he's super attractive. And I'm not normally attracted to men that age."

"You mean men my age." Looking at me over the rim of the wineglass, he eyes me.

"Well, yeah. But Carlo's different from you. Like *way* different."

"Anyway . . ." It's obvious that he doesn't want to talk about his friend. *And I shouldn't either. But here I am, wanting to talk about him.*

I know it's wrong to talk about a man who's about to get married, so I change the subject. "It's been a while since I got choked up about Mom, but it happened today." I've always been able to talk to John about my mother. He's really the only person I have to talk to about her. I know keeping my feelings bottled up isn't healthy, so I have to let it out sometimes. "You remember when we took that trip to Italy, right? Just me and Mom."

"Yeah, I remember. Dad sent you two off on an adventure for your eighteenth birthday present. You didn't want to come back home either." His grin tells me he remembers it perfectly.

I never understood why I couldn't have stayed in Italy. "So, can you tell me now why I couldn't stay there? I was of legal age. There was a woman who was going to give me a job and a place to live at the bed and breakfast she ran. And there was a very cute guy there too."

"And that's why you didn't get to stay." The twinkle in his eyes makes me wonder if he's telling the truth.

"It had to be more than that." I can tell when he's teasing.

Scooping more food onto his plate, he goes on, "Your home is here, Bella. It has been since you were two and your mother brought you here after your father died."

I knew the story well. "Your father and my mother had dated back in high school, and as soon as he found out that she'd lost her husband and had a little girl, he came to her rescue and took us both in. He treated me like I was his own child. Not long after, they got married, and your father adopted me legally, changing my last name to Conti."

"That's right. And I fell head over heels in love with my baby stepsister. The rest is history. See, you belong here, with us, your family."

"But there's not a family here anymore. Not like a real family with a mom and dad. The warmth I used to feel every time I came into this house is gone." John does all he can, but he can't replace our parents. "I guess I'm really beginning to miss them and the way we all were. And I suppose I've thought a time or two about how my life would have been if I had stayed in Italy and made a life there with that cute local boy."

Tears well up behind my eyes. I feel a hand on mine and look up to see John eyeing me with empathy in his big brown eyes. "Bella, I know you're lonely. It's not gonna be that way much longer."

"How do you know that for sure?" I don't even have a guy I'm dating. How can he know that I won't be alone forever?

"I just know. Life won't pass you by. You'll see. You were meant to be with us, the Conti family. One day, everything will fall into place, and you'll understand why you're so important to our family. Even with our parents gone, you are still very much a part of a family."

I wish I had the faith he does. But I just don't. "And if I never find anyone and end up alone, then what?"

"I don't want you to worry about that happening to you. You're important. Don't ever forget that. You have a purpose in this life. You're on the verge of greatness and don't even know it yet."

"With the wedding planner career?" I'm hopeful that it'll take off and I'll be able to fully support myself instead of living off my stepbrother's money.

"Sure." Going back to eating, he leaves nothing on the plate before getting up to take our plates to the kitchen. "You cooked, so I'll clean. Maybe you should go take a nice, long, hot bath. That might cheer you up some. Tomorrow is another big day of wedding planning at Carlo's. You want to be well-rested for that."

Just the thought of getting to see Carlo again excites me, and I jump up and rush to my room to grab my things before taking a bath. There's so much I want to do before the morning comes—

I want to check out some websites about planning the perfect wedding.

It takes no time to get a bath going, and I settle into it, allowing myself to fully relax. John's right. I need to be well-rested. I can't let anxiety get to me. I have to focus on what's important, and that's giving Carlo and his fiancé the wedding of their dreams—Even though neither seems to have any dreams about weddings at all.

I really want to meet this woman.

A man like Carlo Vietti seems like he would be attracted to a feminine woman. A real softy who would love to plan her own wedding. Instead, it sounds like he's marrying a woman with a career that's more important to her than he is.

And with the wedding so close, why wouldn't she be in town, at the very least? And what about her family? Surely, they want something to do with the wedding.

With more questions than answers, I submerge my entire head under the water and try not to think about business that's not mine.

Carlo can love anyone he wants. If he wants to marry a woman who isn't really right for him, then he can. He's rich and probably powerful too. And if he wants a loveless marriage with a career woman who can't even take five minutes to spend time with him, then he can most certainly do that.

If it were me, though, I would be there with him, making the decisions together. And I would want to make plans for a honeymoon too. A great one where we could fall in love with each other all over again.

If they're even in love right now. It doesn't seem like they are. The way he looked at me, held my face in his hands, and talked to me, it seemed like he didn't even remember that he's engaged.

But if he wasn't engaged, I'd be all over that man!

Chapter 3

Carlo

"My little sister has a crush on you," John lets me know.

"How sweet." Smiling, I take a bite of the shrimp linguini I ordered. It fails to even come close in flavor to the one my chef makes.

John, never one to demand much from the food he eats, has an appetite that won't quit. Because his role in our organization is as a protector and enforcer, it's good that he's on the beefy side. His size alone is intimidating.

"The whole planning a wedding for a bride who doesn't care enough to at least help out is making her think you deserve someone better." His laughter is deep, and I can tell he's enjoying this little charade.

Marriage in my family's organization has never been about love or what anyone deserves. It's about keeping bloodlines pure or making alliances with rivals. In our case, it's about showing power and exactly who holds that power.

I hadn't told John the news yet and cleared my throat before starting. "Word came to me that Daniel Barone has begun a search for his long-lost daughter."

John slams his now-empty mug of beer down on the table, making the entire thing quake. "Why the fuck would he be doing that now? After all these years, why now? Do you think someone in our camp leaked our plans?"

"I'm not sure. I have our guys working on it. God help anyone who works for me if they discussed any of my plans. You know betraying me means death. And not a very nice death either. Torture, pain, and more pain are in store for anyone who goes against me. In the end, they beg for a death that comes only when I allow it."

John's been with me long enough to know the way I do business. He gives me a curt nod. "I can't imagine anyone close enough that knows about the plan who would ever double-cross you, Carlo. But if I hear anything, I'll let you know."

"Of course you will." After taking a sip of the subpar wine, I place the nearly full glass on the table. "You know we can't let him find her."

"I know that." He pounds his fist against his palm. His aggravated expression says it all. "That fucker picked an odd time to begin searching for a girl he never gave two shits about before now. He must have some idea that he can use her against one of his rivals." He breaks into laughter. "Too late!"

"Still, we have to make sure she's secure. She's working on the wedding at my place right now. You need to go get her car. Make some excuse about needing to get the oil changed or something. I'll send her home with one of my guys. And I'll have them stay and keep an eye on things through the night." I can't let anything happen to her now. We're so fucking close. It would be disastrous to lose her now.

John knows the drill. "I'll keep her close. She won't ever be alone. Not that she'll be aware of it."

"Keep it covert. I don't want her upset in any way." Already, I felt protective of her. "She's going to have a lot to deal with once it happens. I'm not about to let that motherfucker get to her. Barone has been a pain in my ass, and my father's ass before that. With the marriage, he'll see who has control. I wish I could see his face when he gets the news. It's going to eat his ass up."

"To be a fly on Barone's wall that day would make me very happy. He's a monster. A real, live monster who preys on women and children and destroys innocent people's lives. He has some bad shit coming to him."

I couldn't agree more. "It will be my great pleasure to be the one to bring hell down on that beast. He gives men like us a bad name. It's time his reign comes to an end—and a tragic end would make me very happy."

"My father will enjoy seeing that man taken down." John's smile, sly and devious, makes me smile. "If it weren't for Daniel Barone, things wouldn't be the way they are."

"We did what we had to do to keep her safe. Your father and stepmother have shown where their loyalties lie. I have never known such bravery and selflessness as I have with your family, John. I'm proud to call you my best friend." With a man like John on my side, there is no way I can ever lose.

Leaning back in his chair, he crosses his arms over his massive chest. "I'm proud to be your best friend, Carlo. It's a privilege to get to serve you and fight for you."

There has never been anyone I trust more than I trust John Conti. I just hope I end up being able to say the same for his sister. "I'm honored."

"Should we move things up?"

My fingertips drum on the tabletop as I think. I don't want to rush things. "The plan was for a month from now. I don't think she's ready."

"She's tougher than you give her credit for."

"Tough?" I don't think being tough has anything to do with finding out that you have to marry someone who's almost a stranger. "I'm sure she's tough. It's her mental health I'm concerned about."

His smile reaches his eyes, and he nods. "You're going to be a good husband to her, Carlo. I have never worried about her marrying you."

"The family isn't always easy to marry into. My own mother was kidnapped from her family, my father's rivals. She was full of anger when she and my father married. They still have a tumultuous relationship. I love them both, but I have never envied their marriage." The idea of having to deal with a woman who hates me isn't my idea of a good time.

John waves at the waiter and orders another beer. "One more." Looking at my full wine glass, he asks, "You want a beer?"

"Yeah. The wine here is terrible." The topic of conversation has ruined my appetite, and I push my plate to the center of the table.

"It most certainly isn't up to par with yours." Picking up the beer the waiter puts down, he holds it up. I grab my mug of beer and rest it against his. "A toast is in order. Soon, we'll be even more like the brothers we've always felt we are."

Clanking my glass to his, I sigh. "To becoming brothers." As I drink the tangy alcohol, I think about his sister. Young, fairly innocent, and completely unaware of her fate in this whole thing. "And to producing an heir."

A pained look makes a brief appearance in his eyes before vanishing. "To producing an heir." We clank the mugs, then take another drink.

Placing my glass on the table, I watch as the bubbles burst when they reach the top of the liquid. "I know this can't be easy for you, John."

"No, I'm fine. I've known this was going to happen for a very long time. She was brought to us for a reason. I knew it meant she would be used and that it would most likely be as a bride and heir provider for someone within the organization. I'm glad it's you. I really mean that."

"My mother says twenty-five is the perfect age for a woman to become a mother. She's very excited about the marriage." I remember my mother was sneaking around yesterday so she could see her soon-to-be daughter-in-law. "I caught Mom stalking her. She thinks she's adorable."

"Your mother will be good to her," John comments. "She could use a mother again. She misses hers."

"Mom always wanted a daughter. She got me instead. Of course, having a boy made my father happy." Chuckling, I think about something my mother said. "Mom told me once that God must be on my father's side because he always got whatever he wanted, and she never got anything she wanted."

Shaking his head, he frowns. "Their marriage is so bad."

"It really is. But I think my mother will finally have some happiness. With Isabella to dote on and soon a baby for her to spoil, she should finally feel God on her side for once." I want to see my mother truly happy. That's never been a thing I have been able to witness—not yet, anyway.

"I guess I need to get going. I want to get her car away from her before she finds some reason to go off on her own. If Barone gets to her, it'll be hell to get her back."

"We can't let that happen." I don't even want to think about what that man would do to his daughter if he got ahold of her. Men like him tend to punish even those who had no idea they were doing anything against him. "It's not like it's Isabella's fault her mother took her and ran from him."

Heading out of the café, John pushes the door open. "Yeah, we know that, but Barone's brain works a lot differently than most. At least, people with sane brains. I think Isabella is safe as long as he doesn't find out who his wife gave their little girl to. And since Isabella's real mother, Esmerelda Barone is dead, she can't tell him a thing."

Stopping at my car, I wonder if the truth will ever have to come out about my involvement in the execution of Esmerelda Barone. "Let's be sure to keep my part in her real mother's death a secret. I think we have a shot at getting along. If she knew what I did, she might hate me. The last thing I want is a marriage like my parents have."

Patting me on the back, John assures me, "Your secret is safe with me. It wasn't only you. I was there too. Orders are orders, and back then, neither of us was in the position to argue with your father."

"Still, she never needs to know. I want to keep the waters as smooth as I can. This is all going to come out of the blue at her. Today, I'm going to ask her to try on wedding dresses. I'm sure she'll think that's insane."

"You got that right. I'm sure I'll hear all about your terrible bride as soon as Bella gets home this evening. At least she thinks you're pretty awesome—but she would like it if you decided where you're going on your honeymoon."

"I hate that I'm going to disappoint her right from the start. Keeping her safe is more important than some trip to an exotic place with romance hanging heavy in the air." But it would be nice if we could just run away for a few weeks, really get to know each other, maybe even actually fall in love.

Laughing to myself, I get into my car, close the door, then focus on the reality of this whole situation. I'm going to become a married man sooner than I thought I would. I'm going to take a young bride, do my best to impregnate her, and pray she doesn't hate me for what I must do.

Looking up at the sky through my sunroof, I say a small prayer. "God, please help me to be the man I need to be for the woman I'll share the rest of my life with."

And maybe let her fall in love with me, at least a little.

Chapter 4

Isabella

Fabric the color of blood floats toward me. "Not that," I say, shaking my head. I sent one of the staff members to find me something from Carlo's bedroom so I could find out what his favorite color is, but blood red isn't what I had in mind. "Is that the dominant color in his room?"

Nodding, the woman drops the sheet on the floor. "It's that or black. And black's not a good color for a wedding."

"Neither is that." Wringing my hands, I feel lost as to what to do. "I can't do this with no input from the couple. I just can't. I'll ruin this for them if they can't communicate with me at least a little." It occurs to me that all of the people working with me also work in the mansion. One of them has to know the bride-to-be. "Anyone here know the woman Carlo's marrying?"

Blank stares are all I see, and then the familiar sound of shoes clicking over the floor fills my ears. As soon as Carlo enters the ballroom, he jerks one thumb back toward where he came from, and everyone who's helping me drops what they're doing and hauls ass.

I can't believe he got rid of all my help. "Really?" I ask, with my hands on my hips.

As he nears me, his eyes move to the sheet lying on the floor. "Why is one of my bedsheets in here?" His dark eyes dance as he looks at me.

"I'm trying to figure out the wedding colors. I asked someone to go find me something from your bedroom so I could get an idea of what your favorite color is. Blood red wasn't one of the colors I had in mind though."

"Use any colors you like, Isabella." He takes a seat at the piano I had brought in, places his fingers on the keys, and begins playing a little tune.

"You play?" My heart skips a beat as I think about sitting with him at the piano for hours on end as he plays, with me singing along.

He winks and says, "Obviously." Tilting his head to the side, he urges me to come sit next to him.

Who am I to deny the man?

My entire body tingles as I sit next to him on the small piano bench. My mind goes to the wedding, and I ask, "Do you think it would be too out there if you played the Wedding March when the bride comes down the aisle? I think that might be super romantic. And, let's face it, this wedding could use some romance."

"Could it now?" Grinning, he begins to play the song, and it's absolutely breathtaking.

I hold my hand over my pounding heart, and tears begin to burn the backs of my eyes as I picture the bride, waiting in the wings and hearing her sweetheart calling to her with the notes of the song. "Can you imagine how full of emotion your bride will become when she hears you playing this song for her to come to you?"

"I can." Leaning his shoulder against mine, he smiles. "You have a romantic spirit."

I blush fiercely at the physical contact. "I think that's what makes me a great wedding planner. I'm so thankful you're letting me do this for you. I'll have loads of pictures and videos to add to my portfolio after this wedding. I just know I'll become successful. And it'll be because you gave me a chance."

Leaning against him, I realize what I'm doing and move over. This is my client. My first real client. I have to set a precedent for myself.

Flirting with the groom has to be something I just do not do. Not ever. So, I have to start right now and hold myself accountable for everything I do.

No matter how attracted to him I am.

"I'm sure you will find success in anything you do, Isabella. You're extremely talented. I feel confident in you planning my wedding." His fingers stop moving and rest on the keys as he looks into my eyes. "I have a favor to ask you."

"Anything you need, I'm here for you." I bite my tongue, knowing that it came out way too flirtatious. "As a professional wedding planner, of course."

"Of course," he says with a sly grin that makes me wonder if he's perfectly aware of the way he makes me feel. "I've had several wedding dresses brought here that I would like you to try on."

"Me?" I ask with a shrill voice as I shake my head. "I could never do that. What would your fiancée think?"

"She wants you to do it. She can't be here anytime soon. It would please me if you would try them on."

The idea of pleasing him is affecting me in such inappropriate ways. I know I shouldn't be trying on another woman's wedding dress, but maybe it's not as bad as I'm thinking it'll be. "You just want my opinion on which one is best?"

"I want you to model them for me." His grin grows, and I can see he's getting a ton of satisfaction out of asking me to do this. "Then I will pick the one I want my bride to wear for me on our special day."

"Model them for you?" I can't take a breath. This has to be a dream. Surely, no other wedding planner in the universe has ever been asked to do such a thing. "I really don't think it's appropriate."

"In this home, being appropriate isn't a thing anyone cares about. So, will you do this for me?" He plays a few notes from the Wedding March. "I'll play for you as you walk to me, modeling the dress."

This is way too much!

Biting my lower lip, I think of what I can say to get myself out of this terrible situation. "I'm probably not the same size as she is. I'm a little curvy. I'm sure your fiancée is perfectly proportioned."

"You're exactly the same size as my bride. They're in the room to the right when you exit the ballroom. I'll be right here, waiting. You won't make me wait long." It's more a command than an observation.

Getting up, I know what I must do. "If you really want me to do this, then I will. As long as the bride wants it too."

"She does." He plays another song as I leave the room to go dress in his soon-to-be wife's wedding gowns.

Mirrors adorn the walls of the dressing room, and three gorgeous dresses hang from hooks on the ceiling. I select the dress nearest me and try to put it on but find it impossible to do on my own. Just as I'm about to put my own clothes back on and go tell Carlo it's impossible for me to do this alone, there's a knock on the door. I let the woman in, and she says, "I'm here to help you dress."

Well, there goes that excuse. Damn!

A few minutes later, I'm in the dress and walking into the ballroom. Carlo is all smiles as he stands from his seat at the piano. "That is lovely."

Turning around so he can see the whole dress, I ask, "Do you think this is the one she'll want?"

"I'll have to see the others, but this one is wonderful. The royal blue lace brings out the blue in your eyes."

"Are her eyes blue too?" I ask since he made the comment about the lace.

Nodding, he waves me away. "Go try on the next one."

I go through the same motions as before, and his eyes light up as soon as I come into the room. He's nodding as he looks at this last dress. I can tell he really likes this one.

Running my fingers over the pearl buttons that bring the bodice together, I ask, "So, it's this one, right?"

"You agree?" he asks as he reaches out to me.

I take his hand, and he pulls me to him, our bodies way too close. He begins moving back and forth in a slow dance. "Can you move freely in it?"

"Yes." I can't breathe, not because the dress is constricting me, but because he's so close, so handsome, and such a good dancer.

He bends me over backward, smiling at me. "This is the dress." Pulling me back upright, he lets me go abruptly. "Thank you, Isabelle."

My skin pebbles, missing his touch. And I know that's so wrong. "I'll go hang it back up."

Turning his back to me, he takes out his phone as I hurry away to change into my clothes. And I silently bitch myself out about my inappropriate thoughts of a man who is engaged to another woman.

Back in the dressing room, I ask the woman who's been helping me, "How come no one knows the woman your boss is marrying?"

"You shouldn't ask things like that. We're taught not to ask questions about things that aren't our business." She's as tightlipped as everyone else around here.

But my curiosity knows no bounds. "You all are so well-behaved. Not that I've been in a mansion before or mingled with the staff who care for the mansion and the people who live it, but I can't imagine that you all behave so appropriately at all times."

"It's what's expected of us. If we want to keep our jobs, we do as we're told." Hanging the dress back up, she turns to ask, "Will there be anything else I can help you with?"

"No. You can go," I say, sensing her desire to leave.

Going back to the ballroom, I find Carlo on his phone, tapping away. Waiting until he's done, I then ask, "Is there anything else you need me to do tonight? If not, I think I'll head home now."

Raising his head, he looks at me without any expression at all. "John took your car today. I'll have one of my men drive you home."

I had no idea John had even been at the mansion. "Why did he take my car?" I ask.

He shakes his head and doesn't seem to think it's something I should be concerned about. His attitude is nonchalant. "He had his reasons, I suppose. He asked me to give you a car and driver while you're working on the wedding. Also, I don't want you going out to buy anything. You can put in orders, and I'll have them picked up."

"Why is that?" I sense something odd but can't put my finger on it.

"Because that's what I want, Isabella. I will see you in the morning when my driver brings you back here." He diverts his attention back to his phone and begins walking away from me. "Have a nice night."

I know the people who work for Carlo aren't supposed to ask questions, but I can't help myself. I want to know so much more than anyone here will tell me. "Carlo?"

Stopping, he turns to me. "Yes?"

Licking my lips, I suddenly feel very nervous. But I have to know. "When will I get to meet your fiancé?"

With a shrug, he turns and walks out of the ballroom, leaving me wondering why everything has to be so secretive. Something else pops into my head, and I brace myself, leaning against the wall to keep my feet underneath me.

Am I in a dangerous situation here?

Chapter 5

Carlo

Seeing Isabella in the wedding dresses pleased me in ways I didn't understand. I saw my future in her gorgeous eyes. I saw our future children in her eyes. I saw the woman I'm going to be with for the rest of my life, and I was happy with the idea of spending our lives together.

We have amazing chemistry. Not that I can act on that yet. Soon, the time will come when we can be together. I just hope the lies she's been told so far don't get in the way of what we have.

My cell vibrates in my pocket, and I pull it out to see John is calling me. With a quick swipe, I ask, "What ya got?"

"You haven't sent Bella home yet, have you?"

"She's still here." I have the gut feeling that something's happened.

"Good. Keep her there." Tension riddles his voice, so I know something has gone wrong. "We ran into some of Barone's guys. And it wasn't good."

Deep in the pit of my stomach, I know Isabella's real father has a good idea of where she is and who has had her all these years. "What does Daniel know?"

"Not everything. Not by far. But he's on the right track," John lets me know.

Hearing the sound of the door opening behind me, I turn to see Isabella coming out of the ballroom. I can't let her leave now. "Hang on, let me call you right back." Ending the call, I shove the phone into my pocket as I go to her. "There's been a change of plans."

Her brows arch in question. "Okay."

"The wedding has been moved up."

Casting her eyes to the floor, she sighs. "Okay. How long do I have to get things ready?"

"Less than twenty-four hours. The wedding will be tomorrow." Knowing this is going to freak her out, I add, "You can have as much of the staff as you need. Just get everyone going on this."

Her jaw hangs open. She's clearly stunned. "How am I going to do this?"

Placing my hand on her shoulder, I give her my most confident smile. "I believe in you, Isabella. If anyone can pull this off, it's you. I have a cousin who's a florist. I'll have my assistant text you all the phone numbers you'll need to get things done."

She begins to lose focus, stammering, "I . . . I . . . can't . . ."

Tightening my hand on her shoulder, I try to pull her back to what's really important. "Hey, listen to me. This won't be that hard. For starters, since it's become a rushed thing, there won't be that many people here. Plan for fifty, max. I have some things to take care of, but when I'm done, I'll come to you and help with anything you have left."

Her eyes brighten as she begins to relax. "You'll come help? You'll tell me what you want? And what about your fiancée? Will she be coming tonight to help too?"

"I'm not sure. Maybe." It's not a total lie. My fiancée will most definitely be there. Only she has no idea she's the one I'll be marrying in the morning.

"But I'll have you," she says with a nod. "I can do this. Fifty people isn't many. I can put this together—with lots of help." She spins around and heads back to the ballroom, set on making the wedding work even though I've made it extremely difficult for her.

Heading to my home office, I call John back. He answers, "Hey, I'm on my way to you now."

"Great. Meet me in my office. And you should know that I've made the decision to have the wedding in the morning. Before noon tomorrow, Isabella will be my legal wife. I can't give Daniel Barone any chance of taking her. Even that asshole knows that if he even attempts to kidnap my wife, it will mean war. A war he cannot win."

"So, you told Bella about this?" John asks, sounding concerned.

"I told her she has to stay here and get things finished so we can have the wedding tomorrow. I didn't tell her everything."

"Okay. Well, I'll be there soon, and we can talk."

An hour later, I'm sitting in my office when John comes in. He takes a seat on the sofa opposite me, huffing with aggravation. "Someone has to have been talking about Bella. Barone knows too much."

"What does he know?" Leaning forward, I fill a whiskey glass then slide it to John across the coffee table that separates us.

Taking the glass, he drinks it all down and then places it back on the coffee table. "His thugs didn't tell me much. But they did threaten my life. They said that the truth is out there, and I will die."

Leaning back, I stretch my arm along the back of the sofa. "The truth is out there," I murmur, contemplating what that could mean. Aside from the fact that Barone knows about Isabella and how the family took her in after her real mother's death. "Do you think it was a chance meeting that had you running into his men?"

With a slight chuckle, he shakes his head. "Are there any chance meetings between men like us?"

I know what he means and shake my head. "You were followed."

"Yeah. I had three of our guys with me, so I know they were following me long enough for them to get twice as many men on their side before they came out of the shadows to make their threats." He refills his glass, then leans back and takes a sip. "I don't think they know she's here or about our plans for her. But I know they want her back. And they know I'll protect her with my life."

Running my fingers over the soft fabric of the sofa, I think about the situation at hand. "Right now, they think you're her only protector. But she's really under my protection. Once they know that—and we will make sure everyone knows that by tomorrow evening—the search for her should end abruptly."

His chest rises and falls as he sighs deeply. "Yeah, I'm not so sure about that, Carlo. See, on my drive over here, I made some calls to see what the little birds I have flying around town might've overheard. Talk of overthrowing the Vietti dynasty has been thrown around. And none more talkative about it than Daniel Barone."

"This can't be new," I growl. "How come I haven't heard about this before now? Shit like this has to be squashed before it can gain any momentum." My jaw is so tight I can barely speak. "Do we know who has sided with Barone?"

"Not yet. I'm sure there are some though. We have the numbers to defeat the Barone family without any need to ask your other families for help." But the look in his eyes tells me that's not the case.

"You and I both know that more families will fall in with Barone. The Viettis have monopolized the tri-state area, and there are plenty of organizations who wish they had bigger pieces of the pie." I know what they're planning now. "If they can dwindle our numbers, that will be enough for them to take over some of what we run."

John's furrowed brow gives notice to the confusion roiling inside his mind. "What I can't understand is why Barone wants Bella after all these years."

A horrible idea pops into my brain. "One of his rivals must want her. You know, he pays for their support with his daughter. Someone has set eyes on Isabella, and that's what has sparked the war Barone plans to bring down on the Vietti dynasty." The idea makes my blood boil.

"Has it been that obvious that Daniel's daughter has been alive all these years?" Shaking his head, it's clear he thought no one had a clue about Isabella. "Did he purposely allow her to live with us, only to take her back one day?"

"I don't think it's that cut and dry. Daniel knew his wife was executed. But he knew nothing of their two-year-old, where she was, or if she was alive or not. I'm certain of that. If you'll recall, Barone made threats to many where his daughter was concerned. He knew his wife had betrayed him by running away and taking his daughter with her."

John adds, "He had placed a death warrant on his wife's head. He got that too. We sent him that much. He had no concern at all about who had done the deed of killing his wife. But he did care about finding his daughter."

"I'm sure word got out through the years that my family dealt with his wife. He had to have known that we also had his daughter. He just waited until he had a need for her before he came looking."

"We were owed something for our trouble of dealing with the man's wife. It was your father, who ran the family at that time, who made the decision not to tell Barone the price we charged for keeping his wife's blood off his hands." John runs his hand over his beard, agitation riddling his face. "If he'd been honest . . ."

Feeling the need to caution him before he says something he'll regret, I remind him, "Questioning even a boss who is no longer a boss can result in terrible consequences."

With a nod, he says, "I meant no disrespect, Carlo. It's not like I know what might've happened anyway. The fact is that back then, tensions were high, and anything could have happened."

"That's precisely why we kept Isabella instead of giving her to her father. We knew that we would need her one day." Drumming my fingers on my upper thigh, I think about what might happen. "There are options. There are always options. I could send her into hiding the same way I did your parents when their lives were at stake."

"She's too young to spend the rest of her life being kept in a proverbial dungeon. It would ruin her," he advises me. "You can better protect her as her husband. And her life will be substantially better as your wife."

With all that's going to happen, the idea that we'll find happiness anytime soon is a pipe dream. "She'll find out the truth, and our union won't be as blessed as I'd hoped."

"She'll come around. I know her." Shifting his position, he smiles. "Plus, you have me in your corner. I'll be the voice in her ear that keeps telling her how lucky she is and how this should be like a dream come true since she's had a crush on you since the day you two met."

He has more confidence in her forgiveness than I do. "I knew going in that any marriage I had would be difficult. That's the way it's always been with men who have held the position I do. Why should I get to have it any better than any of them did?"

John's eyes light up. "You forget that Bella has been groomed by our parents to be a subservient woman. She'll fall into line quickly."

"Ah, but she has her father's monster-like blood running through her veins. She might try to kill me. I know her father would love that."

Will I be able to fully trust the woman who will soon be my wife?

Chapter 6

Isabella

Although I'm trying my hardest not to let anxiety get to me, it's proving impossible with the insane deadline for the wedding. "Can you just put the bows on the chairs for me?" I hand the ribbon to one of the staff members who's come to help me. "I need to make sure the wedding arch is coming along.

Just as I begin to walk away, I spot a tall figure entering the ballroom from a side door. It's Carlo, and he's holding up a bottle of something. "I've brought libations!"

He's in a great mood.

Why wouldn't he be? He's about to get married to the woman of his dreams—I suppose. "What have you got there?" I ask, seeing two short glasses in one of his hands and a bottle of some type of liquor in the other.

"Glenlivet. Thought you and I could have some while I show you how to direct others to do the work while you relax."

Looking at the people who scurry about, trying to get everything done perfectly, I know I can't leave them to do it all on their own. "There's just too much to do for me to sit around and point instead of actually doing something." The idea was nice though. "When's your bride going to be here?"

He shrugs, then takes a seat in one of the chairs we've already decorated with bows and ribbons. "Come, sit." He places the glasses on the chair next to him, fills the glasses with the expensive scotch, then holds one up, offering it to me. "Seriously, Isabella, come and sit with me."

Thinking he must want to finally put his two cents into the wedding, I take the glass and take the seat next to him. "You're the boss."

"Yes, I am the boss. Glad you remembered that little fact." Holding his glass up, he clears his throat in an effort to get me to hold my glass up too.

"Oh, you're going to make a toast." I hold up my glass and wait for him to speak.

"To a wonderful future." His eyes sparkle under the overhead lights. He moves his glass closer, and I tap mine against it.

"To a wonderful future." As I take a sip, I find the smoothness of the drink amazing and sip a bit more than I normally would. "This is delicious. I had no idea scotch could taste this good."

"I look forward to introducing you to all kinds of things you've never had before." His smile dazzles me. Then he reaches up and pushes a lock of my hair away from my face.

I can't help but find it odd that he's talking about the future with me being a part of it. "You plan on keeping me around? Are you about to offer me a permanent place on your staff, Carlo?"

"No." He takes a sip of his drink, then looks at the drink in my hand and wiggles his dark brows, urging me to drink too.

It's delicious, so I indulge myself. "I shouldn't be drinking. It's going to be hard enough staying up so late to make sure everything is perfect."

His eyes scan the room. "It looks great to me. All it needs is a bride and a groom, and we're all set."

"It's far from being done." I can't expect him to understand how perfect everything has to be. "I'm trying to make sure your future wife is captivated by her wedding."

"She will be." He takes another drink while his eyes stay on me.

"Tell me about her," I say, thinking he must want to talk. Surely, he's feeling nervous about the fact that he's going to get married very soon. "What made you fall in love with her?"

"She has a good heart, for one thing." He looks away, his expression becoming vacant for a moment.

I can't imagine what he's thinking about. It most certainly has to do with the woman he's marrying never being around. His marriage will be a lonely one if she continues choosing her career over her marriage.

"My mother always told me that things in one's life must be prioritized in order of importance." I smile as he turns his attention back to me. "What is your order of importance, Carlo?"

Raising his head while jutting out his chin proudly, he proclaims, "Family."

"That's the way my mother raised me as well. And within the family, there are prioritizations." My eyes burn as I think about my mother and all the wise things she told me. "Mom was old-fashioned compared to my friends' moms. She thought in old-world ways. But I have to admit that not only did I find her ideals to be important, but I believed in them too. And I still do."

One dark brow rises, and a lopsided smile makes him look young and adorable. "Please tell me what you believe, my young Isabella."

"My mother told me that there is a hierarchy within a family. First, above all else, the marriage is to be honored. It is the matriarch and the patriarch who not only create the family, physically speaking, but make the rules that the entire household must abide by. So, priority number one is to your spouse."

Shaking his head, he laughs. "That's an outdated conception, my sweet girl. Each person should have the same top priority, and it should not be another person—it should be yourself. If you can't be true to yourself, honor yourself, and treat yourself with respect, then you can never give those things to anyone else. Not your spouse. Not your children. Not even your pets. Number one priority? Put yourself first."

"That sounds selfish." I sip on the drink and wonder if he's right and my mother wrong. "Is a mother supposed to put herself above her children?" I think I've found a valid argument.

"Of course."

I know men and women see parenthood in very different lights, but I can't stop my eyes from rolling. "Spoken like a man. Any good mother puts the needs of her husband and children first."

"That would leave her as the *last* priority. Why would anyone do that to themselves?" He takes a drink, draining his glass, then takes mine and fills them both before handing mine back to me. "I like this spirited conversation we're having. I feel the alcohol has loosened your tongue." He snaps his fingers. "Leave us."

"They can't!" I begin to argue, but he puts his finger to his lips. Lips that look as if they have been chiseled out of rose-colored marble but feel softer than goose-down pillows.

"They're already gone." He reaches out his hand to gesture to the now-empty ballroom. "Let's put this theory of mine into practice, shall we? You have worked many hours today. You must be exhausted. Yet you keep working. Why is that?"

Laughing, I answer his ridiculous question. "Because you hired me to do a job. You are paying me to do a job. And I won't be paid unless I do the job. That's why I keep working even when exhaustion begs me to stop."

This time, his eyes roll, and I think he must be drunk if he sees my work ethic as anything but self-prioritizing. "You don't feel that you should tell me to go fuck myself?"

"As if I would ever do such a thing!" I say with a laugh, understanding now that he's drunk.

"You should have told me those exact words when I made an unreasonable demand of you." Leaning forward in the chair, his eyes somewhat glassy, he whispers, "If I had told you to go up to my bedroom and undress, then lie on my bed and wait for me, what would you have said?"

Heat jets through my body as if the sun lit up inside me. "Carlo!"

"Answer my question." His lips firm, he looks directly into my eyes. "What would you have told me?"

Measuring my reply, I know that even if he's drunk, he's still my boss, and I must not disrespect him in any way. "I would have told you that you are going to become a married man very soon and must be feeling the pressure of that. I would have said that, while flattered that you would want me in that way, I would never disrespect you or your fiancée or your impending marriage in any way. And then I would have removed myself from your sight so that you would no longer be tempted by me in any way."

His shoulders droop forward, and that lopsided smile comes back. "You are an angel."

"Not at all. I'm a woman who has respect for the sanctity of marriage. I'm also a woman who wants to be paid for the work I do, and if I sleep with my boss, the chances of me getting paid go way down. And my chances of being killed by his wife go way up."

He nods and gives a one-shouldered shrug. "You might be right about that."

"I think I am right about that." Feeling a tingle of numbness on my lips, I feel I'm on the verge of becoming tipsy and put my glass down. "I've had enough."

He picks the glass up and holds it out to me. "Not yet. I want to make another toast."

"I don't know. I try not to drink past my limits." And going past my limits around him seems like the worst idea ever.

"I insist." He continues to hold out the glass, so I take it. "Good."

Holding it up, I ask, "So, what are we toasting now?"

He's quiet for a long moment before saying, "To you, my sweet, sweet Isabella. May all your dreams come true."

I can't help but smile at his kind gesture and add my own, "To you, Carlo Vietti, a wonderful man who deserves a loving wife. I hope you get what you deserve."

To my surprise, he doesn't drink. He still holds his glass in the air, looking at me with worry in his dark eyes. "Maybe you shouldn't wish that on me."

Unclear why he would say such a thing, I try not to make a big deal out of it. "Hey, it's just a toast. Not some prayer or anything like that. Let's drink," I say in an attempt to lighten his sudden dark mood.

We both drink, and then he places his glass on the chair beside him. "If I made a confession to you, would you hate me for doing it?"

"Carlo, I would never hate you. You're my stepbrother's best friend. I know you're a good man. And no one is without sin. What I'm trying to say is that we all make mistakes." The alcohol has taken over my mouth, and my inhibitions are abandoning me at a rapid pace.

"I like you, Isabella." I try to say something to stop him from making a confession he will regret, but he places his finger against my lips. It leaves them tingling even more than they already were. "I want you."

He moves his finger, and my lips part to tell him something along the lines of he shouldn't want me because he's engaged to another woman whom he'll be marrying in less than twenty-four hours. But that doesn't happen at all. "I want you too, Carlo," I confess without remorse. The woman he's supposed to marry hasn't given him an ounce of her attention, as far as I know. He deserves better than her.

His hands run up my arms, over my shoulders, and then he cups the back of my neck, angling my face before his lips barely touch mine, increasing my need for more. And then his kiss turns from soft to ravenous in an instant, his mouth on mine, taking control like an expert.

My inhibitions are out the window, and I don't care about anything except him and me and how we're going to do things we will both regret and might be a little ashamed of. But, by God, we are going to do them.

This has to be a dream!

Chapter 7

Carlo

Her body melts with my touch, and her mouth yields to mine. She is perfection. Passion surges through me, needing more from her than I imagine she's even ready for. But I'm going to push her to her limits anyway.

Moving her backward until her back hits the wall, I pull my mouth from hers, look into her fire-filled blue eyes, then spin her around to face the wall, yank her dress up, and rip her panties off her, baring her plump ass.

All I can hear is how heavy she's breathing as I run my hand over her creamy white ass. Using my other hand to unbutton my pants, I free the beast, then press my erection against the small of her back as I lean in to whisper in her ear, "I'm going to fuck you now."

Her hands smack against the wall as she prepares herself for my intrusion. Her head is turned to one side, her cheek flush with the wall, and she bites her lower lip with worry of what is about to come.

I adore that she doesn't ask any questions, doesn't beg me not to fuck her, and just lets me do what I want with her. She has no idea how this memory will be burned into her memory bank for the remainder of her life.

The night I took what was mine, and neither of us ever looked back.

Turning her to face me, I lift her up and then bring her down on my hard cock. Her face shows the pain she's feeling as her pussy stretches to fit me. Then it relaxes, and she smiles and opens her eyes. "That feels good."

I find everything about her exciting, and lust takes over. Crushing her mouth with mine, I kiss her as hard as I fuck her. My fingers dig into the flesh of her ass as I hold her up, using the wall to help keep her in place as I pummel her with an intensity that I'm positive she's never experienced before.

She's not a virgin, but her tight pussy tells me she hasn't had much sex. The things I will teach her might boggle her mind, but she will learn every way there is to please me.

Every cell in my body is on high alert. I feel her hard nipples as they rub against my chest with every thrust I make. Her hands move over my shoulders, and then she holds onto me as her body quakes. She cries out, "Oh, shit! I'm coming! Oh, God! This is insane!"

My cock fights to hold back as her pussy goes even tighter around it, clenching it in pulsating waves, trying its best to get me to release my juices into her.

"Not yet," I growl between gritted teeth as I hold back, not about to give in to my desires.

Slowly, her orgasm wanes, and she rests her head on my shoulder, her body soft and hot. "Wow. That was . . ."

"This isn't over." Lifting her up off my cock, I lower her until her feet settle on the floor, then step back. "On your hands and knees."

Fear fills her eyes, but only for the briefest of moments, then she smiles and does as I've told her to. I move the dress that's fallen to cover her pristine ass, then smack one cheek, making her squeal with delight.

As I tease her with the tip of my cock around her asshole, I love that she doesn't try to bat me away or tell me not to go there. I'm not going there—just testing the waters for a future sexual excursion.

Leaning over her, I push her shoulders to the floor, making her ass rise higher so I can get to her sweet spot with ease. Holding my cock, I guide it into her still-tight pussy and groan with the way it holds me in its sweet embrace. "You fit me perfectly."

Her sigh is sexy and primal and ignites a fire inside me. It lets me know she's loving this as much as I am. Moving slowly, I undulate, watching my cock disappear into her and then come back out, slick and shiny with her juices.

When I slap her ass, I can feel every move it makes on my cock inside her, sending vibrations all around it in the best way ever. The sounds she makes send me into a frenzy, and I move faster, wanting to take her to the edge.

Just as I feel the beginning of her orgasm, I pull out. The whimper she makes fills me with happiness. I want her to miss my cock being inside her. I want her to want me in a way she's never wanted anything in her life.

Backing up, I kiss my way down her back, then over her the hot flesh of her ass. Her moans of desire make it hard for me to hold back, but I hang on and keep kissing her body slowly and softly.

She stays in the position I put her in until I turn her to lie on her back. Her hair's a mess, her makeup streaked, and her lips tremble as I look down at her, moving my body over hers, then forcing her legs apart before I move in, filling her cunt with my enormous erection.

I brush her hair from her face and can't stop looking into her eyes as I fuck her slowly. "You are beautiful, Isabella."

Reaching up, she cradles my face in her hands. "You are too, Carlo." I see a tear slip down her cheek. "I know this is wrong . . ."

I can't let her talk about that, so I kiss her to stop the negative train of thought. This isn't wrong, and by tomorrow afternoon, she'll fully understand.

"We're here now, me and you, no one else. Let's just be together and not think about anything other than us and tonight." I want to be easy with her right now.

She gives me a slight nod and then closes her eyes, allowing herself to let go with me and not think about the aftermath of the things we're doing. Not that there will be anything bad, but she doesn't know that.

The element of this being taboo makes it that much hotter. This will be the only time there will be that aspect to the sex we have.

After tomorrow, she will be mine legally, and sex will be very different.

This woman will now be the only woman I will ever have sex with. And, for some insane reason, I'm okay with that. I thought it would be difficult for me to commit to one woman, but this is coming easy for me.

"I could do this forever," I whisper in her ear, then nip her earlobe. I kiss a line down her neck, then bite and suck a spot to leave my mark on her.

"Forever," she echoes with a scratchy voice that sounds sexier than it ever has.

She has no idea what life holds for her. And I love that she's completely unaware of that as we make love for the first time. Her body will crave me forever. We will have a happy marriage with a passionate sex life. I'll make sure of that.

Kissing my way to her mouth, I play with her tongue, and she plays back. The way her hands smooth over my back sends chills through me. Her touch is magical.

I feel her moving her hands over the same places on my back as if trying to memorize every last muscle so she can keep this memory alive, kept forever in a special place inside her mind.

I smile as I think about how she must be thinking this is the one and only time we'll be together like this. In a way, I envy her for that. How exciting to think that you have stolen a moment that no one can ever take from you but can never happen again. To think you have gotten a secret piece of someone that no one else will ever find out about must be exhilarating.

Playing into the idea that this is the one and only time we will ever get to do this, I pull my mouth from hers and ask, "Is there anything you would like to do?"

Her eyes open slowly, a puzzled look in them. "Like sexually?"

"Yes." I can't stop looking into her baby blues. She's so gorgeous and seems unaware of that fact.

She looks to one side, staring at the wall for a moment before turning back to me. "I've never been on top of a man." I find that hard to believe, and my expression must show it because she laughs and takes my face in her hands. "Carlo, I've only had sex a few times. So far, what we've done is far more than I did the other times."

Rolling over with her, I keep our connection intact as I position her on top, then put my hands behind my head. "There you go. What will you do to me, you sexual goddess?"

Blushing, she ducks her head, making her long hair flow down, the soft strands tickling my chest as they move back and forth over it. "I suppose I will ride you like the stallion you are." Leaning back, she begins moving in slow waves that feel amazing.

Watching her fuck herself on my cock, I get lost in the sight. With her eyes closed, her face a mix of passion and excitement, she has to be the most beautiful woman I have ever seen in my life. I have seen many beautiful women, but Isabella is a true beauty. Her soul radiates goodness and kindness. Her sex is filled with movement that stimulates both of us. I doubt she has a selfish bone in her body.

I can't keep my hands off her anymore and move them to take her by the waist to hasten her slow pace. My cock aches, needing to set my seed free.

The friction becomes hot, and her juices begin flowing as her body gives up the fight and let's go. Her orgasm tugs me into the abyss, and then I burst into her. "Fuck!" I growl as I come.

"God!" she screams as her body milks me for every last drop it can get.

When I open my eyes, I can't stop staring at her body, glistening with sweat, her breasts heaving as she tries to catch her breath. Tears run down her cheeks in rivers.

I want to tell her the truth. I want her to know that this isn't the only time. But I can't do that. She wouldn't understand. What I have to do isn't a thing I want to do. But it has to be done.

Lifting her off me, I lie her back on the floor before getting up to get the pill out of the pocket of my pants. It's what's best for her right now.

Her hands cover her face as she cries softly. She doesn't see me when I place the pill between my front teeth and cover it with my lips.

Going back to her, I move her hands, lower myself over her, and kiss her deeply. So deeply that she doesn't even notice when the pill leaves my mouth and goes down her throat.

Sweet dreams, Isabella.

Chapter 8

Isabella

"Isabella?" I hear a man ask.

I can't see well. Everything is blurry, and I feel like I just woke up. "What?" I ask the man whose voice I don't recognize at all.

I wonder if I'm in the hospital and if the voice belongs to a doctor. I don't remember what happened to me at all.

Feeling a hand on my arm, I can tell it's a man's hand, and the way I'm leaning against him, I know he's holding me up. When I look up to try to see who it is, all I see is a blurry blob.

"Do you promise to cherish and obey this man?" the voice asks me.

"Um . . ." I'm not sure what to say. But I figure this has to be a weird dream, so I go along with it. "Yes."

"Carlo, do you promise to cherish this woman for the rest of your life?" the man asks.

Smiling to myself, I understand things perfectly now. I'm dreaming, and the dream is that I'm marrying Carlo. And when he answers, "I do," I laugh.

I hear others laughing behind me and turn my head to find lots of fuzzy blobs. They become a little clearer after I blink several times. My vision improving, I turn back to Carlo and find him looking at me with a stern expression.

I hear a man clearing his throat and see that a Catholic priest is standing in front of us. "Isabella, do you take this man to be your lawfully wedded husband?"

"This is crazy," I whisper to myself, but I nod. "I do."

The priest looks at Carlo—and so do I. He asks, "Carlo, do you take this woman to be your lawfully wedded wife?"

He looks at me with smoldering eyes. "I do."

"You may exchange rings now," the priest says.

I don't have a ring to give, and I look at Carlo with frantic eyes. He points, and I turn around. A young girl stands behind me with two rings on top of a pillow. "Oh, hi there, sweetie," I say.

She smiles sweetly and holds up the pillow. Carlo takes the ring meant for him and hands it to me before picking up the one he's going to give me.

My mouth goes dry as I realize that the ring thing is just about the last part of the ceremony. I grip the ring in my fist as Carlo holds out his hand. It's time to put a ring on his finger.

This seems so unreal, and I'm shaking as I slide it on his finger. "With this ring, I thee wed." My voice is soft and cracks nervously.

He presses his lips against my forehead, and I'm instantly calm. Taking my left hand, he slips a ring on my finger. "With this ring, I thee wed."

My knees go weak as I think about being married to the man I have been crushing on, and I utter the only word I can think of, "Cool."

The priest clears his throat again. "Yes, very cool. I now pronounce you man and wife. Carlo, you may kiss your bride."

Giggling as Carlo moves in for a kiss, I stop as soon as our lips meet. Memories are beginning to flash in my mind.

The two of us, kissing in the ballroom. Naked in the ballroom. Having sex in the ballroom.

Holy shit!

Carlo's arms hold me steady as our lips part, and he turns us to face the people who clap and cheer. The priest's voice comes from behind us, "Allow me to introduce you to Mr. and Mrs. Carlo Vietti."

It seems real. Too real. Not like a dream at all.

But this can't be real. It has to be a dream. All of it. Even the sex.

Carlo leans in to whisper in my ear, "Come, Mrs. Vietti, let's greet our wedding guests."

"Carlo?" I ask, then stop myself.

He nods. "It's okay, Isabella. This will all make sense soon."

"I'm your wife?" I don't understand how this happened. "Me?"

"It was always you, Isabella."

I planned my own wedding?

I have so many questions that I don't even know where to start. Scanning the ballroom full of wedding guests, I don't see my brother. "Where's John?"

"He's late," Carlo tells me as he leads me down the aisle I must have had to walk down all alone.

"He didn't walk me down the aisle?" I can't believe he wouldn't show up for my wedding.

Carlo nods. "We can talk about this later. There's a video of the whole thing. I didn't want you to never know how this whole thing went."

"I'm so confused," I say and turn to find some woman beaming at me.

She reaches out and pats me on the shoulder. "I can't wait to talk to you."

"Me too." I have no idea who she is, but I have a feeling she's someone important.

Carlo's words help me understand. "You'll have a lifetime to talk to your daughter-in-law, Mother."

"Oh! Your mom!" Nodding, I keep looking at her as Carlo leads me away.

So many things begin coming to my mind as it becomes clearer. So many questions. The main one is why I feel as if I woke up in the middle of my wedding.

My wedding!

Why didn't Carlo just tell me I was the one he was marrying? And why did he marry me anyway? Why me? Who am I?

I'm a nobody. And he's a somebody. I don't know who he is, not really, but he's someone that I'm not in the same league with. And what did my stepbrother know about all this?

John's not here, so maybe he didn't know a thing. "Do you know if John's on his way?"

Carlo shakes his head as he stops us in front of the wedding cake I ordered. "I've been busy, Isabella, so I haven't talked to him. I thought he was coming. But I'm sure he has a good reason for missing our wedding."

"Yeah." I don't know why he would miss our wedding, but I don't know a lot of things right now. "So, we're cutting the cake now?"

"You planned this whole wedding," he says as he looks at me with a smile in his dark eyes. "I would think you would be acutely aware of what happens from here, baby."

"Baby," I echo and shake my head. "This is so weird."

"We'll talk later," he whispers, then looks up at our guests. "Are you guys ready for some cake?"

Cheering, our guests flock to watch us cut the cake. Carlo takes the knife and hands it to me. We cut the first slice together. Feeling him behind me this way feels familiar, and a scene comes to mind—the two of us naked, me on my knees, shoulders against the floor of this very ballroom, and him behind me, penetrating me with his enormous cock. I blush as heat surges through me.

My God, what all did I do?

The next thing I know, Carlo is feeding me a piece of cake. I feed him next, and everyone cheers. When he kisses me, we both have cake in our mouths, and it's a pretty delicious kiss. I wrap my arms around his neck to keep him close—I don't want the kiss to end.

Wrenching his mouth from mine, he wipes some frosting off my lips and puts it into his mouth before kissing the tip of my nose, making our wedding guests cheer some more.

Putting his arms around me, he leans in close and says softly, "We're going to have a happy marriage, baby."

Staring into his eyes and having no idea why I'm agreeing with him, I say, "Me too, babe," and then kiss him again.

Kissing him feels right. It feels like something we have been doing forever. Being in his arms feels right. Everything about this feels right.

But it can't be right.

Being forced to marry someone isn't right. Being drugged so you don't fight while being involuntarily married isn't right. Nothing about this is right.

So why does it feel right?

The next thing I know, Carlo takes my hand and leads me to a table full of presents so we can begin opening the mountain of them. "Present time, baby."

I don't know what to say. I have so many questions, but I can't ask any of them right now. You just don't go asking your new husband a lot of questions about how something like this happened in front of wedding guests.

A few young girls line up to hand out the presents. I'm given one to open, and another is given to Carlo. One of the girls takes the card from the gift I'm unwrapping and announces to the guests, "This is from Mr. and Mrs. Dante Vietti." She places the card on the table and watches as I hold up a crystal vase.

I have no idea who the people are who gave it to us, but I smile and say, "Thank you, Mr. and Mrs. Dante Vietti. I love it."

A young woman waves and says, "I picked it out. Keep it in your bedroom." She looks at Carlo. "And you keep fresh flowers in it for your beautiful bride, Carlo. Show her every day how much you cherish her and your marriage."

"That's so sweet," I gush and smile at the woman I have never seen before in my life. But her last name is Vietti, like mine is now, so she must be part of my new family. "I can't wait to get to know you . . ." I give Carlo a questioning look, hoping he'll tell me her name.

Thankfully, he understands and says, "Sofia."

"I can't wait to get to know you, Sofia. I'm sure we'll become good friends." Handing the package to the girl who gave it to me, I turn my attention to the present Carlo holds in his hands. "Your turn, babe." I find it funny that I'm calling him babe, like we've been together for a long time when that's not the case at all.

The girl who handed him the present reads the card, "This gift is from Mr. and Mrs. Giovanni Vietti."

"Let's see what my cousin has given us," Carlo mutters as he begins to pull the white wrapping paper off the box.

A woman calls out, "Isabella, I'm Gio's wife, Grace. I can't wait to get to know you."

"Me too." I feel so welcomed.

Obviously, I've never thought about how it would be if I were forced to marry someone and the whole thing was done secretly, but I doubt I would have expected to feel so good about the ordeal. But somehow, I do.

Carlo pulls a set of fluffy white handcuffs out of the box and looks at the man sitting next to Grace, who must be Giovanni. "Really, Gio?"

The man shrugs slyly and says, "In case she tries to run."

My heart stops. I realize everyone must know I'm being forced to marry Carlo, and some of them think I might try to run away. But then Carlo laughs, and I realize it's a joke.

"Are you going to try to run from me, baby?"

"Never, babe." I shake my head. "But we can make good use of those anyway." I wink at the man he called Gio. "Thanks, cousin."

The gifts have all been opened, so I get up from the table, thinking the event is over. My dress brushes up against the table, shifting the white tablecloth aside a little, and I see something under the table. Bending down, I find a box wrapped in scarlet red paper with no card attached. Holding it up, I ask, "Does anyone know who brought this gift? The card's missing."

No one claims ownership of the gift, so I place it on top of the table and proceed to unwrap it, thinking the card must be inside. As soon as I get the paper off, I smell a familiar scent and smile. "I think it's from John." It smells like the shampoo he uses.

Carlo comes to stand behind me, placing his hands on my waist as he watches me open the box. At first, I don't understand what I'm looking at. "A wig?" I look over my shoulder and see an odd look on Carlo's face.

Still not understanding, I reach in, grab the hair of the wig, and pick it up, finding it heavier than a wig should be. The wig is attached to something. When it spins around to face me, I see what looks like the head of a mannequin. Thick red liquid drips from it and splatters off the edge of the table onto my white wedding dress. Looking down, I see blood puddling at my feet.

Carlo reaches out and takes the thing from me as I begin screaming, "No! No! No!" It cannot be! It can't.

What the hell is happening?

Carlo's grim expression turns to fury as he holds up my stepbrother's severed head. "This means war!"

Chapter 9

Carlo

How dare they! Daniel Barone has gone too far.

I place my best friend's bloody head into the box my wife just pulled it out of. I know that someone from Barone's camp is in my home, and I know what I must do. Isabella's safety is my priority, so I scoop her up into my arms and rush to take her to safety.

Chaos breaks out as the people in my organization realize the same thing I have and rush to get their families out of the mansion. Daniel has brought war to the Vietti family, and none of us will stand for it.

Crying hysterically, Isabella buries her face in my chest. "John! No! Why?"

"Shh," I try to hush her. "I need you to be quiet." She has no idea the danger she's in. But it's time for her to find out.

Carrying her into my saferoom, I kick the door shut, and it locks automatically behind us. The room is outfitted with a bed, some other furnishings, and enough food and water to last a month.

After setting Isabella down on the bed, I can see how upset she is. Looking around, she asks, "No windows? What is this place?"

"It's a safe room. No one will get to you in here." Smoothing her hair, I try to comfort her.

"Me?" she asks with a whimper in her voice. "Are you afraid someone is after me?"

"There are people after you, Isabella." She begins freaking out, and I hug her and try to calm her down, but I understand she has to get some of this out before she can think straight. "Go ahead, cry. Get it all out. I know you're hurt and afraid."

Pulling away from me, she looks at me with a tear-streaked face. "I need to know everything, Carlo. Why you married me. Why the secrets. And why my stepbrother, the only family I have left, is dead."

There are so many things to tell her that it's hard to know where to start. But I have to start somewhere, so it might as well be from the very beginning. "You are the daughter of a powerful Mafia boss who lives here in New York."

Shaking her head, it's clear she doesn't believe me. "No. That can't be right. My mother would never have been with a dangerous criminal."

"Your mother isn't who you think she is. The woman you think is your mother isn't."

Her mouth drops, and she sniffles. "What the hell are you saying, Carlo?"

"Your real mother is dead."

"I know she is. So is my stepfather. And now my stepbrother is dead too. Who the hell cut off his head? Why the hell would they do something so barbaric?" Shaking, she wraps her arms around herself. "I don't understand anything, and it feels like I'm going crazy. Like clinically insane."

I run my hands over her shoulders and wish I knew how to comfort her. "Listen to me. Your father is Daniel Barone, and he's the one responsible for John's murder. The couple who raised you isn't dead. Your stepfather retired, and they're living in Florida."

The pupils of her eyes shrink rapidly, and I worry she's about to pass out. She reaches out and hangs onto my arms. "This can't be true. Why would my mother leave me?"

"She and your stepfather were my associates and had to get out of the business for their own safety. Your real father was getting close to finding out where you've been living. Your adopted parents, the Conti couple, had to be moved, and you couldn't go with them, or their lives would have still been in danger. John stayed to watch over you."

Some clarity begins to filter in. Isabella asks, "Is my real mother still alive?"

And here comes the hard part. "Keeping her alive would have meant that my family would be in danger. She really wanted your safety over everything else anyway. That's why she took you and ran away from your father. She knew she could never go back to him, and she knew she couldn't live within our organization. She knew what would happen to her. It was you she cared about more than anything else."

Her face pale, Isabella asks, "What was my father going to do with me?"

"He would have done what any man in his position would do with their daughter." The grim reality isn't easy to voice aloud, but it's important for her to know. "A daughter is nothing more than a pawn to be used for a variety of purposes. Your mother didn't want you to become the property of some man the way she did."

Her eyes move to rest on mine. "But that happened anyway, didn't it?"

"I would rather you not look at it that way. It's true that I married you to gain some leverage with your father. But the main reason I married you today is to put you under my complete protection. As my wife, you are untouchable by anyone. Even your father."

Strength suddenly forms where none had been, and she sits up straight. "He killed John. Why did he do that?"

"Your father learned that John had you. His life was threatened yesterday, which prompted the urgency for us to get married. Your father wants you back in his possession, and he was ready to kill anyone who got in his way. He will continue to kill to get you back."

Her eyes, vacant, move to the floor. "Give me to him. I don't want anyone else to die over me." Her chin juts out fiercely. "Do it now before anyone else gets hurt. Please."

"I can't do that. I won't do that." I caress her cheek. "Your courage is respectable. But you're mine, Isabella. No one takes from me. And I give nothing away that's as important to me as you are."

She shakes her head and wipes the tears from her eyes with both hands. "Carlo, this is the only way. I can't let anyone else die."

"It's not going to happen. Forget about it." Sitting on the bed next to her, I wrap my arms around her and kiss the side of her head. "You're mine, Isabella. You are precious to me. But even if you weren't, even if I hated you, I would never hand you over to anyone."

"Because that would be an act of weakness, and you would never show anyone that you can be weak," she mutters quietly. "People will continue to die because of me, and you will allow that to happen." Pushing on my chest with her hands, she looks into my eyes. "You are a monster. You're every bit as evil as my real father is, aren't you?"

She's been through a lot, so I keep my temper in check. "Don't ever call me a monster again or compare me to your father. I am nothing like that man."

"Tell me what you are, Carlo." Her body, rigid in my arms, makes me worry that our marriage might not be as happy as I thought it would be.

"I am the boss of all bosses. In short, I am the head boss in an organization that's as old as time and has a vast reach. You can think of me as a king. And you are the same as a princess. Now that you're married to me, that makes you a queen. Can you understand your value now, Isabella?"

"I'm no princess. And I certainly am not a queen. I don't want to be either," she says firmly. "Let me go, Carlo. I don't want your hands on me."

She has been through a lot, so I let her go and stand up in front of her. "I'm giving you some time to gather yourself, Isabella. You didn't know any of this, and I know what's happened has to be mind-numbing. But I am your husband, legally and in the eyes of God. You are mine, and you will behave as I expect you to. Do you understand me?"

"Why did you have sex with me last night? Why did you make me fall in love with you? You could have simply taken me as your wife and never given me the idea that you cared for me at all. Maybe this would be easier to take if I knew the plain truth about it all." Sighing heavily, she leans back on the bed, clasping her hands over her stomach.

I know it's a lot to take all at once, and I never meant for it to happen this way. Lying down next to her, I want her to know the truth. "I didn't care about you, at first. John asked me to get to know you a bit before marrying you. He thought the idea of getting you to plan the wedding would be a good way for us to get to know each other."

"So, my stepbrother was behind this the whole time," she says as she nods. "He's in the Mafia too."

"He was an enforcer." The thought of John being dead makes me angry again, and I have to stand up. "And that bastard took his head. He has to pay for what he's done. Murdering my right hand is almost as bad as murdering my wife. He can't get away with it."

Sitting up, she massages her temples. "I am the wife of a Mafia boss. I came from Mafia, and I have married Mafia. I am Mafia."

"I'm glad you're coming to terms with this so quickly. Maybe your pure blood makes it easier for you to accept what you really are. A Mafia princess who has become a Mafia queen. People will look to you for help from now on."

"The Mafia doesn't help people," she scoffs.

"We help many people. We might make our money from things a little on the illegal side, but we use that money to help those suffering in our communities. You'll see. We're not all bad. But, like anything powerful, some bad things come along with the good things we must do."

I want her to know how I really feel. Kneeling in front of her, I take her hands in mine and run my finger over the wedding ring I placed on her finger only hours ago. "I might not have cared for you at first, but I began to care for you. And then, along the way, I fell for you, Isabella. Last night, things started one way and ended another. I began by fucking you, and then I ended up making love to you."

Her eyes begin to glisten, and she finally smiles. "I remember that clearly now. I felt the shift between us. Had I known the kind of man I was with, I wouldn't have let myself do any of that. Marrying a monster has never been a dream of mine."

Angry that she won't stop thinking of me in that dark light, I rise to tower over her, giving her an idea of the power I have over her. "I am your husband, and you will *not* refer to me as a monster again." As angry as I am right now, and knowing it's better for her if I walk away, I leave her alone.

Chapter 10

Isabella

He left me alone. After all I've been through today, he just walked away and left me locked in a room by myself.

Angry, I get off the bed to investigate my surroundings. I find a small bathroom with a sink and wash my face to get rid of all the salty tears I've cried.

Still in front of the sink, I dare to look at my reflection in the mirror. My eyes focus on the white wedding dress with blood splatter all over the front. "This is what a Mafia queen looks like."

"It's not always this bad," comes a feminine voice from behind me.

Spinning around, I see one of the women from the wedding and recall at once who she is. "You're his mother. Of course you'd think that way."

She holds up a clean dress. "I brought you something to change into." Jerking her head toward the shower, she adds, "I'll wait while you shower and get changed. Take your time, dear."

A shower might do me good, so I follow her advice and take a long, hot shower to rid myself of the horrors of the day. My stepbrother's blood stained my dress, but there is dried blood on my skin as well. It mingles with the water, running off my body in pink rivulets.

Leaning my forehead against the tile wall, I try to slow my breathing. I can't even think right now. This has to be a terrible nightmare. I can't have married a monster. I can't have *come* from a monster. I can't be in this situation.

I get out of the shower, dress, and run a comb through my wet hair. After finishing in the bathroom, I find my mother-in-law still in the bedroom sipping a glass of red wine.

She nods and fills another glass for me. "Come sit at this little table with me, dear. We should get to know one another."

With a shrug, I sit down and take the glass from her. After all, I don't have anything else to do. "Hi, I'm Isabella," I say, "the daughter of a Mafia boss—something I just found out when my Mafia boss husband informed me my entire life has been a lie." Holding up the glass, I add, "So, here's to being the queen behind the king of all that's evil in this world."

She laughs, takes a drink, and says, "He's not as evil as you make him out to be. Many people love my son. His generosity has earned him the respect of many people. Yes, he has had to do some things that might be considered evil, but he did them for the right reasons. You married a good man, Isabella."

"Have I?" I ask and take a long drink of wine. I'm not so sure I should believe this woman. "You're his mother. I think you *have* to believe he's not a bad guy."

"I know my son." Reaching over the table, she places her hand on top of mine. "He wants a happy marriage with you. I know that if that's what he wants, then he's willing to do whatever it takes to make sure you're happy. So, what are you going to do to make sure *he's* happy?"

Shrugging my shoulders, I say, "I guess I could kill a bunch of kittens for him or something horrifying like that. Is that the kind of thing he would like?"

She scowls, and I can see that she doesn't see the humor in my words. "You know you're being a bitch, right?"

Apparently, she likes to get right to the point. "Is that something he'd like? Me being a bitch?"

"Not at all. He has liked you so far. This new side you're showing isn't as appealing, I'm afraid." She bites her wine-stained lower lip, hums to herself, then adds, "You've been through a lot, but maybe you can try to snap yourself out of this funk you're in."

I don't understand these people at all. "I'm sorry. Am I supposed to take in stride the fact that my life is being turned upside down, my world is being shattered, and I just found out that I'm the spawn of a monster and a saint? Is this something all Mafia people deal with on the regular?" After downing the rest of my wine, I slam the glass down on the table. "Hit me again, Mrs. Vietti. I would like to become drunk."

She sighs and eyes me as she refills my glass. "Okay, you get to be upset by what you've found out. But you don't have to take it out on Carlo. After all, he's not responsible for you being born. And he didn't have to marry you. He could've had any woman he wanted—literally, any woman in the world—but he picked you, Isabella. And he married you to keep you safe from whatever your father wants you for. You should be thanking him, not calling him a monster."

"Why didn't he pick another woman? Why me? I don't get it."

"You're of pure blood." She taps her long, perfectly manicured nail on the table to emphasize her point. "Sure, there are others of pure blood too, but you needed protection. When he heard that John's life had been threatened, he rushed to marry you so that he could declare an act of war if you were harmed by anyone. That's pretty fucking romantic if you ask me."

I have to wonder if this woman knows anything about real romance. "But he didn't really do all that for me. He did it for himself."

"How so?" she asks with a smirk, leaning her elbows on the table.

"He told me that I belong to him. He didn't do anything for me. He did it all for himself. He did it so he could get even more power than he already has. What will I get out of this?" I cross my legs and then smooth out the dress, realizing it's the same color as my eyes. "Did he give you this dress to give to me?"

"Yes. And to answer your other question, you get to live is what you get out of this. You get to live a life others would love to have. You'll live in a mansion. You will drive only the best cars. You'll travel in chauffeur-driven limousines, on yachts, and in private jets. You'll eat foods others can only imagine getting to eat. You'll drink the finest wines and liquors and wear designer clothing. Anything you want, you will get. Get it now?"

The frightening thing is that she really seems to think that's what every woman would want. "Sounds like I'll be kept like a prize poodle. I mean, sure, I'll have all that. But only when my keeper, who is my husband, wants me to have it."

"Not at all. You have free will and freedom."

I honestly can't believe she's so brainwashed. "As far as free will goes, I don't have that. You say I have free will, yet here we sit, locked in a room. I told Carlo to give me to my father. I don't want anyone else to die because of me."

"He can't do that." She waves her hand and rolls her eyes at me. "Do you have any idea what that would do to him?"

I would think she would jump at the chance to have me sacrifice myself so others in her family wouldn't die. "Make him look weak?"

"Well, yes, it would make him look weak." Picking up the glass, she takes another drink before adding, "But mostly, losing you would destroy him. If you haven't noticed, he's grown quite fond of you."

"He's fond of his bright and shiny new toy, is all." I know I mean no more to him than any other object. Men like him have no real connection to anyone. They can't feel love for anyone or anything because they fear it will be used against them. Hence the reason he married me—merely to get to my father.

"You know nothing about my son. He's never acted the way he has since meeting you. I think he actually loves you, Isabella. And if you could stop being a bitch, you might find that you love him too." She smiles at me like a cat who ate the canary.

"Are you enjoying calling me a bitch?"

"Not really," she says with a frown and actually looks like she means it. "I would much rather call you sweet names. From what I saw of you before you found out your life has been a lie, you seemed very sweet and accommodating. It's like a switch went off that turned you from good to evil in an instant. Just because your asshole father's blood flows through your veins doesn't mean you have to be as negative as he is. You had a mother too. And she was caring and selfless."

Astounded that she brought up my real mother, I have to ask, "You knew my mother? My real mother?"

"She came here to see my husband. She came to her husband's enemies to get help for you. You were about two then. Cute as a button too. Your mother knew what would happen to her, and she came anyway. She knew you were better off with us than you were with your own father."

"Why didn't you and your husband take me?"

"That would be way too obvious. We're in the spotlight. He was once the boss that our son is now. So, we gave you to one of my husband's trusted associates, the Conti couple. No one had any idea of the Contis' dealings with the organization. Plus, you would have been considered Carlo's sister. That wouldn't have worked out at all."

"I was two. There couldn't have been any idea of him marrying me back then."

Tipping the wineglass, she took a drink and then said, "There was some idea of it. You were a Mafia princess, after all, and very valuable. And at that time, Carlo was a Mafia prince."

"That's disgusting." Shuddering, I realize I have no idea what goes on in the Mafia world. "I hate this whole fucked-up situation."

"You weren't thinking that way last night, were you?" She smiles knowingly at me and wiggles her dark eyebrows. "When you let my son screw your brains out all over the ballroom?"

Holy fuck! Was she watching us?

Chapter 11

Carlo

Once the mansion was cleared, I had my wife taken to my bedroom. Locked away and under guard is the only way to keep her safe. Her anger at me is probably at an all-time high, so I prepare myself for the onslaught that surely awaits me on the other side of this door.

I see the guard smirking. Squaring my shoulders, I turn to him. "This funny to you?"

The smirk vanishes as he shakes his head. "No, sir. You should know she's been banging on the door and shouting that she wants to see her husband."

With a nod, I open the door and step inside my bedroom suite. The living area is a little messy. Pillows have been tossed around the room, and a couple of pictures hang oddly on the wall, having been hit in the midst of her fit.

An empty bottle of wine lies on the threshold that separates the living area from the bedroom. It gives me a glimmer of hope that she's gotten herself drunk and the alcohol has lessened her anger.

Night fell hours ago, and the room is dark. A beam of light from the attached bathroom flows over something blue on the bed. Going to the bed, I find her face down. "Are you awake?"

Muffled words come, but they're unintelligible. She turns over, her face blotchy and her eyes red-rimmed from all the crying she's done. For a short moment, there's a softness in her expression, but it morphs into fury at lightning speed. "You locked me up!"

She launches at me, and I have to grab her wrists to stop her from punching me with her delicate fists. Trying not to laugh at the absurdity of her attempted assault, I adopt a stern expression and say, "Stop."

Her struggle stops, but her eyes bore holes of hatred into me. "Where have you been?"

"Dealing with things. You were locked away and put under guard for your own protection. I will not apologize for that." Letting her go, I give her a moment to calm down.

Which she refuses to do. "You couldn't have come to see me even once in the many hours I've been kept prisoner here?" she asks, glaring at me. "You couldn't spare a moment for your fucking wife, Carlo?"

"I'm only going to warn you once, Isabella," I say, narrowing my eyes at her. She has to understand her place. "You need to watch your tone and what you say to me. You are mine in every way, and I will do whatever I want with you."

Staring daggers into me, she snaps, "You don't own me! This isn't ancient times when men owned their wives. You can't scare me."

She needs a good dose of fear. "This may as well be some faraway kingdom in the Middle Ages for all the rights you have, my dear wife. See, you married a man of the Old World. There is no judge who will grant you a divorce. That's if you ever got enough freedom to get that far in the first place."

Her eyes go wide. "Will I always be your prisoner?"

She might as well know the reality of her situation. "You are valuable, Isabella, and you must be protected at all times. There will always be guards around you, and your whereabouts must be known at all times. It's just the way life is when you're the wife of a powerful man."

She leans back on the bed but is anything but relaxed. "I had no say in marrying you, and I have no say in whether I want to be guarded or not. I've lost all my rights to live a normal life. And all because you had to have me. Me. An unremarkable woman who has never known who I really am."

"Don't sell yourself short. Your blood makes you one of a kind. You and I will make children with an even more remarkable bloodline that, if I have my way, will only become purer and purer as each generation brings forth their own children."

"You make having children sound like some kind of horror experiment." She clasps her hands over her stomach and looks at me with a sharpness in her eyes that I shouldn't allow. "When did blood become something so sought after?"

She has been through a hell of a lot, so I ignore her tone. "Bloodlines have always been important. Your bloodlines go as far back as mine do. Binding our blood will make strong and intelligent children."

Her brows raise. "And if we have a child who is not so strong or intelligent? What then? Will they be given away? Or something worse?"

"You shouldn't worry about that. It's not a good idea to tempt fate. It's important to keep a positive mindset, Isabella. Remember that. Great things will happen for us."

"You have no idea what the future holds, Carlo." Scoffing at me isn't a smart thing for her to do, yet she does it anyway.

Moving with the speed of a rattlesnake, I'm on the bed, hand on her throat, squeezing only a bit. "I warned you to watch your tone with me. You will not disrespect me in any way. Do you understand?"

For a moment, her eyes stare into mine without an ounce of emotion. I need to see fear in them, so I squeeze her throat a little tighter, restricting her air.

Finally, she nods, and I release my hold on her. She moves her hands to her throat as she looks at me with fear. "I had no idea you could be this way."

"And if you knew, would you *not* have given yourself to me last night?" I ask, not expecting an answer. "As you have seen, I can be quite pleasant to be around. It all depends on how you act when you're with me. If you're nice, chances are I'll react nicely to you. If you're a bitch, however, I will be your worst enemy. You're not stupid. You understand. I know you do. All this is a lot to take in, but I trust that you will—and quickly at that. You have a position now. You are my wife, and that means there are certain jobs that will be yours to take care of. Therefore, the sooner you get over the shock of your new situation, the better it will be for everyone."

Blinking, she seems dubious. "Are you saying that I can't be a wedding planner?"

I shrug. It's not like I care if she plans weddings or not. "If that's something you want to do, and someone needs it done, then you can do it. You can't be paid for it, but you can do it."

She cocks her head, obviously uncertain about something. "What do you mean I can't be paid for it?"

"You are the wife of a man who has more money than most people can imagine. It would be a sign of disrespect to me if you accepted money from anyone. My mother will teach you everything you need to know about being the matriarch of this family. It's a prestigious role that you should be proud to have been given."

Looking down, she says quietly, "I don't feel I've been given anything. What I feel is that I've been thrust into something that I never asked for. And it's not fair at all."

"No one ever said life was fair, baby." She's old enough to know that's just a fact of life.

"Your mother doesn't like me." She looks up at me with sad eyes. "She's called me a bitch more than a few times. I don't think she'll teach me anything."

"She'll do as I tell her. And she wouldn't have called you a bitch if you weren't being one. My mother is a straightforward woman. Just like me, she can be your best friend or your worst enemy. It's up to you. I would recommend being her best friend. Her loyalty knows no bounds." My mother is the least of her worries, not that she knows that yet.

"Would it be disrespectful if I told you that I don't want to be this person for you?" Her hands grip the blanket, and she stares at them instead of looking at me.

Taking her by the chin, I tilt her head up to make her look at me. "I was born into this role, Isabella, the same way you were. We all have our parts to play, and I think we have pretty fucking great roles. You should try to see the good in being my wife. You were crushing on me up until you found yourself standing at the altar with me this morning. That attraction couldn't have vanished. I think you can find it again."

"Pulling my stepbrother's severed head out of a box gave me the feeling that being with you is extremely dangerous." Her eyes move rapidly back and forth, searching my own. "Can you try to understand the way I feel?"

I caress her cheek, understanding her feelings more than she knows. "If you were left without my protection, the things your father would do to you would be far worse. He must have someone he wants to give you to, or he wouldn't have begun searching for you. If you weren't with me, then it would be someone else. God only knows who that would be and how they would treat you."

Her jaw tightens. "It's not like you're treating me great, Carlo."

Just as I think she's softening up and beginning to understand things, she says something ugly. Getting up, I pace, run my hand through my hair, and try to think of the right words to say to her to get her to stop being so combative.

"Just leave me alone. Like you have all day." She turns over, putting her back to me.

Not acceptable. I yank her up so she's facing me, tearing the shoulder of the blue dress I bought just for her because it matches her eyes perfectly. "Don't you ever tell me what to do. Not ever." Finishing the job, I rip the top of the dress down to her waist. Her lacy bra is exposed, and I pull it off her, baring her plump breasts.

Her chest heaves as she breathes faster, fear in her eyes. "Carlo, please . . ."

"Shut up. You've said all I'm going to allow you to say. This is your fate, dear Isabella. You will have my children. As many children as God will give us. I will fill you with my seed anytime I want. I will fuck you anywhere and any way I want—and you will shut your fucking mouth and take it. You will bend to my will. You will obey me without question. You can be happy or sad about it. I don't give a shit how you feel. All I care about is getting you pregnant and keeping you that way."

Her lower lip trembles and a tear falls down her cheek. "I hate you," she says with a stern tone.

"Hate me. Love me. I don't care. You're mine and always will be. When we're around other people, you will act as if you care for me. If you don't, then your ass will stay in this very bedroom, and you will see no one but me."

Why does she have to make this so fucking hard?

Chapter 12

Isabella

God help me—why is my body reacting to him this way?

I'm quivering, my heart pounds, and my pussy is soaked. I can barely breathe as he stands over me, looking more powerful than any man I've ever seen. I bite my lower lip to stop from saying anything that will set him off again.

He reaches out, taking what's left of the dress in his hand and ripping it all the way off me. In a swift movement, he tears my panties off too, leaving me naked on the bed.

His eyes hold mine as he removes his clothes. Then he moves over me. His posture, stern and strict, warns me not to do a damn thing he doesn't want me to do—or suffer the punishment.

I don't want to be excited, but I can't help it. My body is on fire, and all I want is to feel him inside me.

He forces my legs apart, then thrusts his erection into me. Even though we were together like this only one night before, my pussy burns as it stretches to fit the length and girth of his shaft. I want to take hold of him, feel his muscles rippling as he fucks me with steady, even, disciplined strokes, but I lay perfectly still.

It seems we're both too stubborn to admit when we've been wrong. Even though his cock feels amazing as it makes deep strokes into me, I still can't make myself apologize. I can't bring myself to say anything.

My body, on the other hand, has a mind of its own, and my back arches up to meet his thrusts. He grinds into me, his face still stern. I'm unable to hold back, and my hands move over the muscles of his back. I take a deep breath, letting the tension flow out as I release it.

Our bodies want each other—there's no doubt about that. The way he moves makes me weak. His handsome face so close to mine makes me want his lips on mine.

I look at his mouth and see his lips coming closer to me. They touch mine, and I fall into the abyss that's us.

My nails rake over his flesh. My anger is expressed as passion. I never asked for any of this, and I hate it. Yet here I am—actively fucking the man who's stolen me.

Digging my heels into his ass cheeks, I try to push him in even deeper. His low groan tells me he's enjoying my moves.

His kiss, hard and demanding, suddenly ends, leaving my lips pulsing and wanting more. He moves, his lips grazing across my neck before biting down hard, making me whimper in pain. The pain turns into pleasure, and the whimper turns into a moan of desire.

My anger crumbles a bit as my body directs me to relax and enjoy my husband's attention. Words flow from the tip of my tongue and out of my mouth in a soft whisper. "I'm sorry."

Holding me tight, he rolls us over, putting me on top. With a smile in his eyes, he whispers, "Me too."

Moving his hands through my hair, he looks at me with something akin to love in his dark eyes. I lean over to kiss him softly, and tears flow as I feel myself losing all the anger I had at him.

It's not his fault, and I know it. He was born into this, and so was I. But he's had a lifetime to get used to this, while I've had only a few hours to come to terms with who I really am.

Moving my lips away from his, I kiss my way to his ear. "I want us to be happy."

He puts his hands on my shoulders, pushes me to a sitting position, and takes my face in his large hands. "I want that too."

"Thank you. I haven't said that, and it needed to be said. Thank you for marrying me and putting me under your protection. I won't take that for granted."

He slides his hands down my sides, his eyes smoldering with desire. "You're welcome. It's my pleasure to take care of you, Isabella Vietti. I will guard you with my life. You have my word on that."

I don't know how it happened. How can I be so angry—and even afraid—and then feel something that's the opposite of those emotions?

This life isn't something I understand completely, and I probably won't for a while. Being the wife of a Mafia king isn't something I ever saw in my future. But here I am, queen to his king.

"I'll try my best to make you proud of me," I let him know. "I know I didn't start out on the right foot, but I'm done blaming you for the lies I've been told my entire life. It's not your fault. None of it is. You've been nothing but good to me, and I owe you my life."

Cupping the back of my neck, he pulls me down to him, kissing me as he turns us back over with him on top. He releases my lips and looks down at me with eyes full of emotion. "I'm proud of you, Isabella. You're strong and not afraid to say what you feel." Chuckling, he smiles. "You're the only person who has ever stood up to me like that."

I run my hands through his thick, dark hair, loving the satin-like softness of it. "I promise not to make a habit of it."

Shaking his head, he says, "If you feel strongly about something, I want you to talk to me about it—but maybe not with as much hostility. Talk to me about things that concern you or things you feel strongly about. You are important, and I want to be able to treat you that way. Of course, that can only happen if we have mutual respect for each other."

"Well said." I run my fingertip over his lips. "You're a wise man."

"I've been through a lot, and wisdom comes with experience. Life isn't something to take for granted. We never know when our last day will come." Leaning down, he kisses one breast and takes the other in his hand, caressing it, tweaking the nipple until it's hard as a diamond.

A low moan vibrates deep in my throat as he takes me back to the deep darkness where we can be one with each other. It's crazy that I can feel so close to him this fast. It makes no sense at all.

Yesterday, I was a single woman with plans that had nothing to do with being married. Now, I'm the wife of a man who brought me to the altar in a drugged state. I should want to kill this man. I should want to struggle against him. I should hate him.

But I don't want to do any of those things.

I want to be happy. I want to live a long life with this man. I want to wake up in his arms each morning and fall asleep in them each night. I want him. I want us. I want this marriage.

Maybe it's my blood that has allowed me to take to this so easily? I don't know anything about the Mafia or the pure blood Carlo talked about. I have no idea what that blood flowing through a person's body means for them. Is it like having a superpower? Or maybe like being a vampire or something evil? My bet is on evil because there is a ton of violence associated with the organization.

My stepbrother's severed head flashes in my memory and brings tears to my eyes. There's so much I didn't get to say or do with him.

Soft lips kiss my cheek, and I see Carlo looking down at me with soulful eyes. "Are you okay?"

Nodding, I wipe my eyes. "I got lost in thought, and John came to mind. It was so sudden and violent, and it's hard to understand. Why did they kill him?"

His lips form one line, and he closes his eyes for a moment. When he opens them, he sighs. "Daniel Barone gave him a choice. Hand you over or die."

The tears burn as they build up again. I've cried so many tears that the well should be dry by now, but somehow, there are still more, and they flow down my cheeks. "I can't believe he did that for me. I owe him so much that I'll never be able to repay."

Kissing my forehead, Carlo whispers, "I owe him too. He kept you alive for me. He knew you and I belonged together and was sure we would get along well. That's why he made the offer when I began talking about taking a wife. He knew my desire to have a happy marriage. He was a good man and will always be missed. I will avenge him, baby. You can count on that. His murder will not go unpunished."

I have never been a tit-for-tat kind of person, but I want something to happen to the people who killed the only brother I have ever known. "I'm glad you're going after them. I don't care if it's my birthfather—I want justice for John. It shouldn't have come down to either giving me to that monster or him having to die. My birthfather sounds like a fucking coward. John was a hero. A real hero. Daniel Barone can go to hell for what he's done."

"I will send him there personally." He kisses me and pulls me close. I can feel the truth in his body.

My new husband treats my body to unknown pleasures. His maturity, experience, and self-discipline have made him an exceptional lover. How lucky am I that he is mine?

We move with one purpose, working together to bring each other pleasure. My body shakes as the waves inside me crest then plummet, sending quakes through my body that make my pussy pulse around his cock.

"Fuck!" he growls as my orgasm takes him along for the ride.

Hot, wet, and satisfying, his cum saturates my pussy. Spent, he falls to the side of me. I lie on my back, trying to catch my breath.

He rolls onto his side and rests his head on his hand. "Our marriage has been consummated," he says, looking down at me. "It's official now. Together forever, baby."

That should sound horrifying, but for some reason, it feels exactly the opposite of that.

Chapter 13

Carlo

A month into the marriage, the mansion is bursting with holiday festivity. Sitting at the breakfast table, Isabella enjoys a cup of coffee with my mother. The two have become friends since Isabella's attitude took a drastic turn on our wedding night.

As I do most mornings, I join them. "There are my favorite girls."

My mother giggles as I kiss her cheek, then move to Isabella, taking her hand and kissing the top of it as I look into her pretty blue eyes. "My lady, you are looking lovely this morning, as always."

"And you're looking handsome as ever, my sweet husband." She pulls me down and leaves a soft kiss on my lips.

A cup of coffee is brought for me and placed on the table before I even take my seat next to my wife. "So, what do you two have on the agenda for today?"

"Decorating," my mother says as she picks up a delicate pastry.

Isabella tells me, "She wants me to add something to the decorations you already have—you know, add my touch for the holidays. But I haven't done much decorating and, to be honest, don't even know what I like."

With a shrug, I pick up my cup of coffee. The steam drifts away as I blow across the top. "You'll just have to do a lot of shopping to figure out what you like. The House of Holiday has everything you could possibly want—it would be a great place to find something."

Mother's eyes light up, and she grins at Isabella. "Would you like to go on a shopping trip today?"

Isabella hasn't left the mansion in a month since we married. Going out should sound like fun to her.

Looking at me, she asks, "Would that be safe?"

"You would be well-guarded." Patting her hand, I nod. "You should go. You two will have a great time. Maybe get some lunch too. Have a real day out on the town."

Isabella chews on her lower lip, her insecurity about going out showing. "Can I think about it?" She looks at my mother, and I can tell she doesn't want to offend her. "It's just that this would be my first time going out since I found out everything about myself."

Tapping the rim of her coffee cup with her long fingernail, my mother looks a little worried. "You can't be afraid to leave the house, Isabella."

I nod. "You can't be afraid of anything. Not when you are who you are. I should've noticed your hesitation before. You need to confront it and move past it. You need to go out today."

"But you didn't want me to leave," Isabella whines. "You told me it wasn't safe for me to leave this house. Why is today any different from the other days?"

Looking at her over the rim of my cup, I wink. "Because I said so. Don't overthink it. Just do it. Go and have fun. You'll be protected by my best men. There's nothing to fear. You know how I feel about fear."

"You abhor it," she mumbles.

My mother is quick to change the subject. "It'll be nice to add your unique personality to the place. I mean, I know it's a mansion, but it's a home at its heart. It's the little touches that make it that way. I started the Christmas village when I first came here. Some of the decorations and ornaments for the tree are antiques that came from Italy, where my husband's parents are from."

Looking at me, Isabella asks, "That means you're what? Third generation American, Carlo?"

"That's right." I look at my mother. "Mother, tell her about her heritage."

"I had no idea your mother knew anything about my real family. Please do." Isabella leans forward with curiosity in her eyes.

"Well," my mother begins as she puts down her cup of coffee, "your grandparents lived in the same neighborhood as my late husband's parents. As a matter of fact, Carlo's grandfather and your grandfather were what some would call best friends."

"That's crazy," Isabella says excitedly. "So, our families were friendly when they were back in Italy?"

Nodding, my mother goes on, "They lived in the city of Palermo on the beautiful Italian island of Sicily."

"My family comes from Palermo, and I had no idea. This is wild!" Isabella gushes.

With a nod, I add, "Our families, once friends, became rivals. Our grandfathers fell in love with the same woman, and that's when the war began."

"And still goes on to this day," my mother says as she brushes a lock of dark hair back into place. "And no one got the girl either."

"What happened?" Isabella asks, curiosity overtaking her. "Did she marry some other man and break both their hearts?"

"Wouldn't that have been a happy ending for her?" my mother asks and shakes her head. "But no, that's not what happened. The men got into a fight, she got in the middle of it, and she was shot. Both men had drawn their guns, and both fired a shot. No one knows whose bullet actually took her life. She died right there in the streets of Palermo as the men who loved her wept openly and held her as she passed on."

"They blamed each other for her death, and the rivalry continued," I add. "It grew and even traveled across the seas when the families brought their budding organizations to New York. Giuseppe Barone and Francesco Vietti were the first of several Mafia kings to come to this part of the world."

"I can't believe the history our families share," Isabella says. "It's astounding. So Guiseppe Barone is my grandfather?"

I laugh at the tone she's used to describe the barbarian. "Don't say that with any pride, baby. He was a very bad man. And he planted his evil seed in your poor grandmother who bore your father. We all know what kind of evil monster that man is."

I can tell that the idea of coming from monsters hangs heavy in her soul.

My mother clears her throat to get Isabella's attention. "Hey, don't let it get to you. It's not like Carlo comes from saints. His father and grandfather weren't exactly angels."

I don't like where the conversation is going and change the subject. "Anyway, I think you should think about your day. One thing I will tell you is that there should be no spontaneity. Plan it all out, and stay on the path you lay out for yourselves. That way, I can have a set of my guys a step or two ahead of you at all times to make sure the way is clear for you."

Shivering, Isabella hugs herself. My mother frowns at her for a moment but then smiles and says, "By this time next year, we're sure to have a baby to share the holiday with. Won't that be nice?"

I expect to see a happy smile on my wife's face but see tension instead. She says, "Carlo, about that. I've been meaning to talk to you. Is there a chance that this thing with Barone will be settled anytime soon?"

My laughter fills the room as I shake my head. "Didn't you hear the story? The Barones and the Viettis have been at each other's throats for three generations. Even if Daniel Barone is taken out, there are plenty more family members who will carry out his vendetta against us."

Nodding, she goes on to say, "We'll never really be safe then."

"You're safe with me, Isabella. I don't want you to talk like that or even think that way. Yes, there will always be a level of danger—it comes with the business we're in. It might help to know that my grandfather died peacefully in his sleep of old age. And my father died from cancer because he smoked cigarettes."

"And John died when his head was removed from his body by my father. People do die, Carlo. Maybe not the big guys like you, your father, and grandfather, but people die. It only cements the idea in my head that bringing a child into this is not only dangerous but criminal."

"Yes, people die." Wrapping my arm around her shoulders, I pull her close and kiss the top of her head. "But they also die in the streets, hit by a bus. They die in wars all over the world. They die in their beds, safe at home. You can't let death get in the way of living your life. We all die sometime."

"I know that's true. But we know for a fact that the way we live is dangerous. I can't shake the idea that having a baby would be irresponsible. Bringing a child into this would not be a good thing for us to do."

"I don't know why you would say a thing like that," I say, narrowing my eyes. "You know how I feel about negativity, but here you are, talking about something that you know I want only positive things said about. Our children are never to be spoken about in anything but a positive manner. You know this."

"But you have to agree that this just isn't a safe time for us. At least it's not for me. You have to understand that *I'm* not really safe right now. What if my father gets me somehow?"

"That's it." I can't let her say any more and clap twice to get a couple of my men to come get her. "Take her shopping. Show her that she's perfectly safe."

"Carlo," she says quietly, "are you sure about this?"

"I am, and I've given the order. Get out for a while with my mother. The two of you will have fun. You'll see. No more worrying. Promise me."

Her eyes tell me she's nervous, but her nod tells me she will do as I say. "I promise not to worry, Carlo."

I can't understand where I went wrong with her. We've been getting along so well this entire month. She knows we're going to have children. As many as God grants us. To bring this nonsense up is unreasonable.

For all we know, she might be pregnant right now. And what would she want to do with the baby if she were pregnant? Get rid of it?

Perhaps it's her that I should be worried about and not her father. Can I trust my wife to take care of herself when she does become pregnant, or will I need to hire nurses to care for her around the clock?

After this disturbing conversation, I need to relax. A nice shave and fresh haircut will do me good. Maybe a chat with the boys at the barber shop will help me understand women and the way they think.

Did she really think I would agree to not having children?

Chapter 14

Isabella

This is not what I wanted.

I'm not ready to leave the house. But what my husband says goes.

This is a Mafia marriage. Women in a marriage like mine have no power. If my husband says I have to have his baby, then that's what I have to do, no matter what I think about it. If he says I must go shopping with his mother, then I have to do it.

I go up to our bedroom to get my purse. I try to be happy about the shopping trip. I'm sure we'll be just fine. Going to the window, I pull the curtain open and watch as the car my husband is in drives away. He never tells me where he's going. He doesn't have to tell me anything. He's the man, and I am nothing but his woman—his wife to do with as he wants.

Leaning my forehead against the cold windowpane, I wonder about the way life would have been had Carlo Vietti not wanted me for his wife.

He told me that my real father had plans for me. For all I know, he still has plans for me. But are those plans any worse than Carlo's?

My eyes go to the bed that we have shared for a month. In that bed, we're nearly insatiable, and neither of us can get enough of the other. Everything else fades away.

We feel lust for each other in spades. What we lack is the mutual respect my husband likes to pretend we have.

Do I respect him? Yes—but I have opinions. Opinions he never wants to listen to.

Still, I must remind myself that our marriage is new, and we have much to learn about getting along and listening to each other.

His mother and I have become pretty close, and the stories she tells of her marriage are more like horror stories. Neither Carlo nor I want our marriage to be bad. I'll try to remember that before I say things that might make him angry with me.

Going downstairs, I meet my mother-in-law in the foyer, where she waits with two of the guards. "Are you ready, dear?"

"I am." Putting my best foot forward, I try to enjoy a nice day of shopping. "I can't wait to see this Christmas store Carlo talked about."

"It's wonderful," his mother tells me as we walk behind the guards. I notice a couple fall into step behind us.

I have to admit that I do feel safe with so many big, burly men around to keep us safe. "This is going to be fun."

Traffic is horrible, as usual, and it takes us over an hour to get to the store. But once we're inside, I'm mesmerized by all the holiday glory I have to choose from. "I'll never be able to get just a few things."

"Get all you want, Isabella," his mother tells me. "No one told you that you had a spending limit."

"I'm not used to that." Turning in a circle, I don't even know where to start. "There are so many things. Should I begin with ornaments for the tree? Or maybe outdoor decorations? I just don't know."

Looping her arm through mine, my mother-in-law takes charge. "Okay, I've got a great idea. How about we get a tree for the living area of your bedroom suite?"

"I can decorate an entire tree?" I like the idea. "I need a theme. Red bows and green lights? Or blue and white ornaments?" With so many themes, it's going to take me all day to find what I want. "I had no idea this would be so hard."

"It's supposed to be fun," she says. "I'll get you started. Think about the colors of your bedroom suite, and let's play on that color scheme. It'll help you get started."

"Red and black," I say as I haven't gotten around to putting my feminine touch on the bedroom yet. But I do find a theme that would fit. "Over there. I see something that would fit in nicely."

"Good. Now we're on to something." We head toward the black and red section of the enormous store, both of us ready to dive in.

Finding everything I want is slow going, and as the day wears on, more and more customers come into the store, searching for just the right thing to make their holidays bright. Before I know it, there are so many people around us that I lose track of my mother-in-law.

Looking around, I see her and wave. She shouts, "I'm going to the ladies' room. Keep shopping. I'll find you when I get back."

I look over my shoulder to see two of the guards nearby and get back to searching for the perfect decorations for my tree. Feeling happy about my finds and looking forward to surprising my husband with the tree in our suite, I think about nothing but the holidays and how much fun they'll be.

Moving deeper into the store, I'm on a roll, finding one thing after another, filling my basket to the very top. There are so many people around that when I feel a bump on one side of me, I think nothing of it. "Excuse me. Sorry."

A bump comes from the other side too, and I turn to see someone wearing all black. Turning to look on the other side of me, I see another person wearing all black.

Just as I start to back up to get out from in between the hefty men, I find they each hold an arm, and I can't move backward. Frantic, I jerk my head around to look for the guards but can't see anyone I know.

"Help . . ." I manage to get out before I'm jabbed in the side by something sharp and a cloth is shoved into my mouth.

Everything becomes blurry as I'm dragged away from my basket full of holiday cheer. Double doors open into a back room that's dark. I try desperately to hold onto consciousness, but the blackness closes in fast.

Daylight flashes as another door is opened. I'm shoved into the back seat of a car that speeds away. One of the men is in the seat with me, and he begins tying up my hands and feet. "Let them know we have her."

Who has me?

The only thing that keeps me from giving up is the fact that my husband is the most powerful man in the city, and I know he will turn this town upside down to find me. And those who have taken me will die horrible deaths.

I have no pity for the people who have dared to kidnap me. I want them to pay. I want my husband to rip them limb from limb for what they've done.

Even though I brought up the danger I'm in and how it might not be a good idea to have a baby right now, I can't be angry with Carlo for sending me out on a shopping spree anyway. I couldn't have stayed hidden inside the mansion forever. This was bound to happen.

When someone wants to kidnap a person, there isn't any real way to stop it from happening. If these people got to me inside a public place with security of its own and the men my husband sent to guard me, then they could have gotten me inside our home.

There is and never was any way out of this situation. Sometimes, things just have to happen. Sometimes, things just have to be dealt with. This must be faced, and these people must be dealt with.

"Text her that we're fifteen minutes away," I hear the man near me say. "Tell her to have the room ready. We'll slip in the east entrance. No one can know she's there."

Although my brain is falling into a deep, dark fog, I know that whoever has kidnapped me has been planning this for some time. It has to be my father.

Carlo will know it's him, and he will come to the Barone mansion and rip up everything until he finds me. He won't stop until he gets me back. And he will kill everyone who tries to get in his way. My father has no idea how dead he is now.

Something about what the man said makes me wonder if I'm right about it being my father who's had me kidnapped. The man said the word *her*. He said to text *her* that they were fifteen minutes away.

Women have no power in the Mafia. None.

I see the man who's driving hold up his cell phone, showing the man sitting with me in the back the return message. When he opens his mouth, I see something odd, and the guttural noise he makes doesn't sound like any words I've heard before.

"What happened to his tongue?" I ask, now seeing it's only a stub rather than a full tongue.

"The boss cut it off when this one said some things he shouldn't have," the man in back with me lets me know.

"Good God," I mumble, fearing the very worst now. "Is that something he does a lot of, cutting people's appendages off?"

The two of them laugh instead of answering my question. I don't like it at all. I don't like any of this. Of course, there's nothing about kidnapping that's designed to be liked.

If the person behind this is my biological father, I really do come from a monstrous bloodline. But I remind myself that the man said *her* and not *him*. So, it can't be my father, and that riddles me with confusion and anguish.

Who would face the wrath of the Vietti family just so they could take me? It can't be a Mafia family.

And that means everywhere my husband looks for me won't be the right place. He'll accuse my father. He'll accuse all the other Mafia bosses. And he'll be wrong.

He might not find me!

The last remnants of light fade. I can't see anything, and what I hear becomes fainter until I can't see or hear a thing as I fall victim to whatever they shot me up with.

Please find me, Carlo!

Chapter 15

Carlo

A visit to the barbershop is just what I needed to smooth out the annoyances of this morning. If a man needs one thing in his life, it's a good barbershop where he can renew and refresh himself, especially when you run the kind of business I do. Luigi has never let me down.

I go up to the bedroom to find no one guarding the door. "Hey!" I call out, but no one says anything back to me. I know they have to be back from shopping by now.

My men know there is always to be at least one man at this door at all times. The fact that nothing has happened to her so far must have had them flaking off. But that won't work for me.

First, though, I want to talk to my wife and go into the bedroom. "Isabella, baby?"

Maybe I was wrong, and they're still shopping. Taking out my cell, I call my wife, but the call goes straight to voice mail. Her battery may have run out, so I call one of the guards I sent with her and my mother.

"Boss, we have a problem," he says when he answers.

I tense up. "Are they okay?" I want that information first because my wife and mother are the number one priority.

"Your mother is with two of my best men. Your wife? Well, we're still searching for her."

What the fuck?

Clenching my fist, I don't hold back my anger as I shout at the imbecile, "Why was she ever alone in the first place?" *Heads will roll for this!*

"The store's crowded. We thought we had her in our sights. Your mother went to the ladies' room, and that divided up the team. Somehow, she just disappeared on us, boss. But we're looking everywhere right now. We're gonna get her back. I don't want you to—"

"Worry?" I ask, interrupting him. "I'm not worried. I'm furious. Her father wants her, and now she's gone. And you know fucking well who's fault that is, don't you?"

The first time she's gone out since the night before our wedding, and she's been taken. She was right—there was a reason for her to be afraid. But I trusted my men to keep her safe. They let me down, and they all know the penalty for that.

"Should I send someone to the Barone mansion, boss?" he asks, trying his best to keep his head since he knows I'm holding him responsible for my wife's disappearance.

The fact he hasn't already done that only pisses me off even more. "I'm coming down there." Fuck these morons. If I have to go find my wife myself, then that's what I'll do.

Anger isn't anything new to me. But anger at this level is something I have never experienced before—and I don't care for it. I just need to get my fucking wife back, take her home, and teach her never to walk away from her security team again.

When my driver pulls up in front of the store, I get out and take long strides to get inside. There are people everywhere, shoppers who have no idea anyone important is missing.

We have to keep it that way, too, so no one of any real importance finds out that my wife is not in my possession. If not her father, there are others who would love to get their hands on what's mine.

This is a dog-eat-dog kind of business, and one has to play their cards close to the vest at all times. So, when one of my men sees me, he nods, acting cool like nothing is going on. "Hey."

I nod back and shove my hands into my pockets as I look around for any sign of Isabella. "Hey."

We separate so we can cover more ground. The first thing I notice is there's a shit-ton of people in this place. It would be fairly easy for Isabella to get out of the eyesight of her guards if she wanted to. I've already spotted ten women with the same hair color and body shape as my wife.

Would Isabella want to leave me?

She knows her father wants her. She might have thought that if she went to him on her own, he might treat her better than if she had to be brought to him.

Looking around the huge store, I see that she could have simply ducked down and used the crowd to hide her. She could have made her way to the exit and left the building.

I don't want to think my wife would leave me, especially since we have been getting along so well in the last month. But this was the first time she's been outside the mansion, and she's gone missing. What else can I think?

For all I know, she might even be pregnant already. She brought up the idiotic notion of not having children yet due to the danger she's in, but perhaps that was some kind of ruse.

I don't know her well enough to know what kinds of things she's capable of doing. I know how she was raised. I know John said she was easy to get along with and naturally subservient. But that was before she knew who she really was. Before she knew she'd been lied to her entire life. And before she knew that she had been raised by her father's rivals and married to his biggest rival of all.

Could she have left on her own? Could she be on her way to the Barone mansion right now? Or am I way off?

Not that it matters. She's mine and always will be. If she does go to her father, asking for his protection, it won't stop me from getting her back. Even that man knows he can't take what's mine—even if she was his first.

What I'll do to her if she did run is another thing entirely. Betraying me and my trust is unforgivable. Most people die for doing something like that. But I suppose I'll deal with that if it comes to it. She might be carrying my baby. Killing her would be out of the question if that's the case.

Maybe I'm making excuses for not wanting to see her dead. Maybe she's gotten to me somehow. Maybe she wanted to fool me into thinking she has real feelings for me and wants to be my wife. I can't put anything past the woman. She is a Barone, after all.

Scanning the area, I find my mother. She sees me and comes toward me. Her face is pinched, and she looks upset.

Approaching her, I look past her at the guard behind her. "She shouldn't be here," I tell him.

"I agree," he says.

My mother touches my hand. "Son, I've been waiting for you." She slips something into my hand. "I can't trust this to anyone else."

It's a small piece of paper, and someone has written a few simple words on it that would mean nothing to anyone else in this store. "Where did you find this?"

"In the basket where she was putting all the decorations," she tells me. "I hadn't thought about it until just a few minutes ago. I went back to where she left the basket in one of the aisles and found that piece of paper under the angel that she was going to put on the top of the tree for your suite."

"Well, there's no reason to stay here. She's gone." I shove the note into my pocket. "Tell our men to meet me in my office. She's no longer missing. I know where she is."

My mother comes with me, holding my arm to help keep her steady. "I'm so afraid for her, Carlo."

"I know you are. But I'll get her back." And many people will die over what's happened here today.

"But in what condition?" my mother asks, looking at me with tears streaming down her face.

Pulling out a handkerchief, I hand it to her. "Wipe away the tears. No one can see you like this. We never show weakness. You know that."

Sniffling, she wipes her eyes. "I know. It's just that I'm so afraid for her. And the thought that she might be pregnant makes it so much worse."

"We'll get her back," I say once more. "And we will deal with whatever we must deal with." And her father will die for what he's done today.

"She must be terrified," my mother says.

"She's strong. Give her credit," I tell her, as well as myself. "She's a Vietti and a Barone. The woman has strength in spades."

Within the hour, I meet with my men in my office at the mansion and have one of them make the call to Barone. With his phone on speaker, we hear as the call is answered. "Hello?" a man asks.

My man says, "Carlo Vietti wants to speak to Daniel Barone."

"This is Darius Stone. I'm his wife's uncle. I'm afraid Daniel can't talk to Mr. Vietti."

"That wasn't a request," my man says. "It was a notice to you and your family. Carlo Vietti will speak with Daniel

Barone—and he knows why. We can do this the easy way or the hard way, but it will happen."

"I'm afraid it would take a miracle for anyone to speak to Daniel Barone right now, or ever for that matter," Darius says.

Sick of whatever game this fucker is playing, I say, "Look, I don't have time for this. I want to meet with him today. He knows why. He can meet me in a neutral place, or I'll come to his home. But I *will* see him today."

"Sorry—I haven't been straightforward with you," Darius says. "The news is being kept quiet right now. But it will soon be out."

"What news is that?" I ask with irritation.

"I can see you think Daniel was behind something. And he may well have been—I'm not one to get in his business. But he is no longer with us."

"Explain that to me," I say.

"He was on his way to mass today when he was assassinated."

"He was killed this morning?" I ask to be sure of the timeline.

"Yes. Around eight," he says.

Anger and fury combine inside me to form what promises to become a volcanic eruption. Walking out of the room, I pound my fist against my palm.

Daniel was dead before Isabella was taken, so he didn't give the order. But if not Daniel Barone, then who?

We're taking her home where she belongs, the note said. It had to have been from Barone. But it couldn't have been if he was dead. Could another rival family have taken her?

Barone won't leave my mind though. Maybe his men went through with his initial order after his death. Maybe they thought the new boss, whoever that will be, would want Isabella as some kind of leverage against me.

But why?

All I have are questions with no answers. This isn't the way I want things to be. I am Carlo Vietti, king of the Mafia, and what I want, I get.

I can't trust Darius Stone. I can't trust anyone from the Barone family to be truthful with me. The note was explicit. Taking her home where she belongs can mean only one thing—she is with the Barone family. But her father is no longer around to lead that family.

Who else in the Barone family could be calling the shots right now?

Chapter 16

Isabella

Where am I?

Everything's blurry as I wake in a dimly lit room I don't recognize. When I try to lift my arm, I feel something heavy slip and hear a clanking sound. Sitting up, I see a chain around my waist that's padlocked to the bedframe.

Closing my eyes, I try to remember what the hell has happened to me. Two men took me from the store. I was stabbed in the side and then began losing consciousness, but I remember being put into a car.

And now I'm here.

One tiny window at the top of the tall wall gives minimal light to the small room. There's the bed I'm chained to, and I see a small bucket on the floor near the end of the bed. I see no other doors, and I assume the bucket is meant to be my bathroom. Wherever I am, they only mean to give me the bare minimum.

Trying not to cry, I hold onto hope that my husband is looking for me. Carlo will kill every single person who had anything to do with this kidnapping. All I have to do is hang on until he finds me.

Leaning my head against the wall, I take deep breaths to calm myself as fear and anxiety bubble inside me. I can't let it get to me. I have to be strong.

Something moves in the far corner of the room, and my eyes immediately go to the area. "Is anyone there?" I can't figure out why someone would want to sit in the shadows and watch me, but there's nothing I can do about it.

I lean back and think about what I can do to help get myself out of this predicament. The first thing I need to figure out is who has kidnapped me. My father is the only one I knew of who had plans to take me.

I take a chance and ask, "Are you Daniel Barone?"

"Don't you dare speak his name," a woman's voice says from the shadows.

"Who are you?"

I watch as a woman's shape emerges from the corner. "I'm your stepmother, Isabella."

She moves closer, and I finally see her. She's an attractive older woman with dark hair and eyes. "So, my father did have me kidnapped."

"Your father is dead," the woman says with no hint of sadness in her voice.

This seems like good news.

"What happened?" I don't even know why I ask when I don't really care.

"He was murdered. Shot while on his way to mass in his limousine. A hitman did the deed." She steps closer. "He wasn't a nice person. He had many enemies. Me included. But I didn't want him dead. Not yet, anyway. His death has left a mess for me to clean up. Starting with you."

"From what I've been told, I haven't been anything to my father since I was two years old."

"Ah, but you are his firstborn, and he never forgot that," she says.

"I know he never forgot about me, but I'm sure he had only bad things planned for me."

"Your father left everything to you, his long-lost daughter. He left me and our daughters out of his will completely." A smirk tugs at the corner of her mouth. "But I have a plan to get what's ours."

The wheels inside my head are spinning out of control. "Are you saying that I'm an heir to my father's money? Well, I don't want it. I don't want any of it. You can have it all."

Shaking her head, she says, "*An* heir?" Her chest rises as she inhales deeply. "No. You are his one and only heir."

"I'll give all the money to you. I swear I will. I'll sign anything you want. What's your name? I don't feel right not calling you by name."

"I'm Vivian Barone. And you can't give anything away. Your father had his lawyers make sure our daughters and I will never get a thing from the estate. It's yours alone."

"But I don't want any of it. All I want is to go back home to my husband. He's not the kind of man who'll take this lightly. I'm positive he's already devised a plan to get even with you. I can help your daughters and probably you too. But only if you set me free. If not, he'll make sure you all die horrible deaths. I don't want that for any of you."

"I know all about the self-proclaimed king of the New York Mafia. What a joke that is." She laughs. "My husband was dead before you were picked up. Your husband has been made aware of that. I'm sure he's looking elsewhere for you now."

This isn't good.

"My husband isn't a stupid man. He might think someone else has me right now, but it won't take long for him to come back to the Barone family. You'll see. But you won't have to face his wrath if you just let me go. I'll protect all of you as best I can. But you have to let me go to do that."

"And what would you do with that freedom, Isabella?" She tosses her long, dark hair over her shoulder and places her hands on her hips. "I'll tell you what you would do. You would run to your husband, and he would take everything my family has worked so hard for all these years."

"I swear to you I won't do that." I don't understand why she won't believe me. "I have no need for money, and neither does he. My husband has more than I can even imagine."

"You have no inkling of the wealth you stand to inherit. But I do. And I know exactly what I want to do with the money. But I have to move fast. There is a power vacuum right now with Daniel's death. While he made sure his money went to you, his power within the family wasn't a thing he saw fit to handle yet, so there's a small window of time before another man takes his place. For now, I'm in control. But that won't last long."

"I'll just give you the money. All this is for nothing, Vivian.

"All I know is that you are the only heir of a fortune that's rightfully mine." She begins pacing and looks nervous. "If you had any idea the torture I have endured at your father's hands, you would understand why I feel I'm owed that money."

All I want is to go home. "Please, you have to believe me, Vivian. I'll give you everything I get."

"The only thing I know right now is that the man I've lived in fear of is dead, and I am finally free. And I want what's mine." She stops her incessant pacing and glares at me as if this is all my fault. "You keep saying you'll give me everything, but the fact is that you won't have any control over that. The control of my husband's fortune will fall into your husband's hands. And I know he won't give me what I deserve."

"You shouldn't have kidnapped me. That was your worst mistake."

"He has no idea I kidnapped you. Like I said, he's been informed of Daniel's death, and I'm sure he's moved on to question other rivals about your disappearance." She begins walking toward the door. "None of this will be easy. It has to be handled very delicately."

"It *is* easy!" I shout, not wanting her to leave. "Please, I beg of you, don't leave me here to die. I will give you everything you want. I can get my husband to agree to it—if you let me go right now. If not, I can't make any promises. If you leave me to die, he will end you all."

Her hand touches the doorknob, then she stops and turns to me, a grim expression on her face. "Leave you to die? You wish it would be that easy for you. You have to stay alive until the will is read and probated. After that, I will end your life." The door flies open, and she leaves, closing and locking it behind her.

I try my best to hang on to the little strength that's left in me. I keep replaying Carlo's words in my head about not being afraid and being strong. "I will *not* be afraid. I will be strong. I will be strong for as long as it takes. I will get out of this place alive and be back with my husband soon. I will live. I will live. I will . . ." A sob interrupts my testament to inner strength.

The woman hates me. She hated my father. And now that I will inherit it all, she wants me as dead as he is.

Vivian is heartless, and those without hearts are the most dangerous kind of people. My father is surely to blame for what his wife has become. Not that this fact helps me at all.

Choking back my tears, I try to pull myself together. I have to stay strong. I can't let weakness bring me down. I have to make it out of this alive. I have to.

A shadow moves over the room, and I look up to see a bird as it flies past the window. I notice the thin branches of a tree and realize I'm in a room that might be on the top level of the home.

Only it's not just a home. I'm sure it's a mansion. My father's mansion. I think I'm in the attic or maybe a space inside the attic.

There must be something I can do from way up here to get someone's attention on the floor below me. Even if they only come up to see what's up here, I might be able to talk them into setting me free—especially when I offer them an enormous bribe to do it.

There may be hope for me yet!

Chapter 17

Carlo

Walking into the breakfast room, I greet my mother. "Good morning, Mother." I take a seat, where a steaming cup of coffee waits for me.

Looking at me with concern, she sighs. "No word of Isabella's whereabouts yet?"

"I know where she is. I just have to bide my time so things can fall into place." I sip the hot coffee, thinking about the hell that's going to rain down on the Barone estate.

"I hate waiting and being constantly worried. I wish I could be like you, so calm and fearless. I didn't sleep at all last night, thinking about where she might be and how she's being treated."

"You must keep in mind that your daughter-in-law is a very strong person. I'm sure she's being treated well. Even the most idiotic people in criminal underworld know that if my wife is treated badly, the things that will happen to their families will be much worse."

"I know you know what you're doing, son. I just miss her and want her home." Dabbing at tears with a napkin, she sighs. "I know you'll have her back here before I know it."

My mother can't be let in on the details, but I can ease her worry. Placing my hand on her shoulder, I smile at her. "Things are happening as we speak. It won't take much longer to get her back here where she belongs."

With my mother feeling better about getting her daughter-in-law back soon, I head to my office to meet with some of my men. A set of blueprints sprawls across the top of my desk. "Nice. You got the plans to Barone's mansion." I walk over to check it out and see that a few rooms have been marked.

"We have a guy on the inside," Titus, my most trusted adviser, tells me. "He's a chef who used to work for us a few years back."

"What's he told you?" I take a seat, and one of the men brings me a cigar and a glass of something strong.

"He's confirmed she's in the house, but he hasn't found out where she is yet. We're sending in someone to help with that," Titus says, then smiles. "He's done work for us before. His specialty is finding those who don't want to be found."

"Sounds like just what we need." I take a hit of the cigar. The smoke I exhale encircles me, and the aroma adds satisfaction to the taste. "I need this done quickly. It won't be long before the new leadership of that family is established."

"By what the chef has said, the man who took the call we made yesterday, Darius Stone, has already had lawyers coming and going through the night." Titus nods at me, knowing that I know why that is.

And I do. "Her kidnapping has something to do with the things her father has left behind."

Titus shrugs. "Maybe Daniel's wife didn't get all she thought she should have. Maybe she wants whatever your wife's got."

"And there's little time left to make sure anyone gets anything with the power about to be given to another man. Daniel Barone had no sons, so the leadership will go to another in that family." I sip on the smooth liquor and think about the males in the Barone line who might take over.

"There's a shortage of males in that family," another of the men says. "There will definitely be some trouble between those who are in line for that position."

"While they're fighting among themselves, the guards at the mansion will be in short supply," Titus adds. "No better time than now to make our move."

"As soon as we know where she is," I say. "I'm not charging in there with guns blazing until I know where she's being held. I want zero chances of her being harmed in the crossfire."

Titus points to the basement, one of the rooms that's been marked. "If she's here, then I'm thinking maybe a car bomb could be set off near this area to give us access."

I look at the attic, which is also marked. "And if she's way up there in the attic?"

"Then we'll need to get to her," Titus says with confidence. "Chaos is a great distraction."

"I do love chaos," I say with a laugh, and the others join in.

The more chaos, the more things we can get away with. It has never failed us before.

I will get my wife back, no matter who I have to kill to make it happen.

Chapter 18

Isabella

The day comes to an end, and dinner is brought to me in my attic cell. Earlier in the day, I was let out of my cell and taken to a downstairs office to meet with the lawyer in charge of the whole estate thing. I had to sign papers that I was sure would lead to my death. They gave me no time to read anything, so I have no idea what the papers said or what I was heir to.

Now that I have been seen not only inside the Barone mansion but also with Vivian Barone, I have a feeling that others are aware of what's going on. And with me being alive and in the care of my stepmother, she can't exactly kill me herself. Still, I know she plans on me dying in one way or another. She can't let me live—that much is clear. And I don't want to die.

To my surprise, Vivian herself brings in my dinner. She's followed by a male figure, and I see who it is as they step into the thin beam of fading light that comes from the window high above us.

I want to scream at them, tell them they will never get away with this, but I clamp my jaw shut. Yelling will only make them laugh, and that will further infuriate me.

After Vivian sets the plate of food at the end of the bed, the two of them step back, clearly afraid of getting too close to me. Vivian smiles. "Today went well, don't you think?"

"You got what you wanted, so I'm not surprised that you feel it went well," I snap.

I watch as the man she's been calling her uncle slides his arm around her waist, pulling her close to his side. She says to him, "Soon we will be rich."

"Um, am I missing something?" I ask. "You two are a little too friendly with each other to be related."

Arching one thin brow, she smirks. "It's none of your business, but seeing as you'll soon be dead, it won't hurt for you to know that the whole story about Darius being my uncle is a farce. I made it up so he would be welcome here. My husband would never have agreed to host this man had he known he was really my lover and not my uncle at all."

It's funny to me that this woman has spent so many years around the Mafia but seems to know so little about it. "Do you think your husband's successor will approve of this? Or are you still going to pretend you're this man's niece?"

Her hand goes to her chest, and her dark brows rise. "Why would you think I'm going to stay here? Once I have the money, we're out of here. And I'll finally get to marry the only man I've ever really loved." She caresses the man's cheek. "Darius and I will finally get the life we deserve."

Under normal circumstances, I would be happy for them. But they kidnapped me, so I feel nothing but anger. "I wish you both the life you deserve," I say, not meaning it in a good way.

My mother was right for leaving with me when she did. She knew what would happen if she'd stayed. She gave her life so I would have a chance in hell of avoiding the horror of my father. Little did she know that it would come back to haunt me anyway.

Leaning over, I pick up the plate from the end of the bed and force myself to eat, even though I have no appetite.

"It's only fair that your poor sisters get to live as nice a life as you have," Vivian says.

"I never knew about them or you," I say. "I was told only recently about who my real father is. As far as my half sisters are concerned, I have no ill will against them. Unless they're as horrid as you are."

"They're angels, despite the abuse their father put them through." She waves her hand in front of her face as if fanning away tears. "You were lucky to have been taken away before you had to endure your father's evil punishments."

"And I'm thankful for that. But I lost my mother in the process. I grew up thinking another woman was my real mom. I was told lies my entire life. Still, I hope you take the money and give your daughters a nice life. Even if I have to die for you to do it, which I still don't think is necessary."

Vivian rolls her eyes and sighs. "I can't have what you have unless you're not around to have it."

She has no idea what fate awaits her, whether she gets the money or not. "Vivian, you are an enigma."

"I have no idea what you mean by that, and I don't care." She looks at me with disgust. "You're enjoying that?"

"Not at all." I finish the food, even though it's bland, and I know it's not what the family was served at dinner tonight. Putting the plate back down at the end of the bed, I ask, "Is there any way you can get me some vitamins?"

Vivian raises her head to look at me. "You need vitamins and nutrients on your deathbed? Why is that?"

"Well, I signed your papers, and you will soon have no choice but to allow me to move about this place. Someone other than the bloodsucking lawyers and a few servants will have to see me if any of your shit is going to be believed." I'm not sure how to say it without actually saying it. "I have to look healthy until I can't be anymore."

"You won't live past tomorrow night," Darius informs me with a chuckle.

"It would be extremely stupid of you to have me killed in such a short amount of time. The blame would be placed on you, Vivian. Surely, you realize that."

"Killed?" she asks, a sinister grin spreading across her ruby-red lips. "There are many other ways a person can die other than being murdered. I'm sure you can think of at least one way."

Darius blurts out, "Suicide!"

"And why would I kill myself? Especially after inheriting a nice sum of money?" I ask, thinking I've never met any people as stupid as these two.

Vivian taps her finger against her temple. "Well, you might not love your new life as a Barone heiress, and that's why you would take your own life."

"But I'm a happily married woman who only wants to get back to her husband." I know that at least my husband will know I wouldn't kill myself. "It's not the police you should be worried about. Something as simple as suicide might fool detectives, but it will never fool the one you should be afraid of."

"Your husband," she says as if he's no real threat.

"My husband is more powerful than either of you can imagine. You're already dead for what you've done. If I die, death will be something my husband will make you beg for. And he'll make you watch as everyone you have ever cared about is tortured in front of you. I'm begging you to think about the things you're bringing down on not only yourselves but your children and everyone else you know."

She gives me another eye roll. "Please, spare me your drama. You think your husband is more powerful than all the Barone men put together? I'm protected by my husband's men and will continue to have their protection even when a new boss is put in charge."

"My husband is not without his own men. I think you've been hit in the head one too many times, Vivian. My father has knocked you senseless. I'm telling you that things don't have to get as bad as you seem set on making them. But you refuse to listen to anything I have to say. You aren't taking me seriously at all, and it will only serve to hurt you in ways you cannot imagine."

No matter how hard I try, she won't see reason. I don't know what else I can say to make her understand what she's doing to herself if she lets me die.

Maybe she thinks my husband doesn't care for me the way hers didn't care for her. But she must know how protective men like our husbands are.

"I was able to get to you with relative ease, Isabella. Daniel had men looking for you for a month, and then he died, but I was able to send men to find you in no time at all. Your husband didn't know of Daniel's death, I'm sure, before he sent you out to shop. If you ask me, he was trying to get rid of you."

I know better than that and refuse to let her get to me. "Let's pretend for a moment that I mean nothing to my husband. What I might be carrying inside me *will* matter. If I die, and he finds out that I was carrying his unborn child, what will happen to you is beyond my imagination."

Her eyes move to my stomach. "You think you're pregnant?"

I can see that means something to her. "I do."

"You and he have been married a month. You can't be sure about that yet." Her eye twitches a little.

"I'm never late, and I was due to start yesterday. It's possible that I'm pregnant. We've been trying as hard as humanly possible to start our family."

The reason I mentioned the idea of not having children until I was out of danger to Carlo was because I was worried about my period being late. When I woke up yesterday without any sign it was about to start, I couldn't help thinking about the possible consequences if something happened to me.

And now it has.

Chapter 19

Carlo

In a meeting with my closest advisers, we're working on the plan to get my wife out of the Barone mansion when my cell rings. Too busy to take a call right now, I toss it to one of my assistants.

He answers, "Carlo Vietti's phone. What can I do for you?"

I run my finger over the blueprint of the mansion. "My inside guy should be getting back to me soon to let me know where my wife is. But my bet is on her being in the least used and least populated area of the home. That could be the basement." I run my finger over the basement area on the blueprint. "Or the attic, like we talked about earlier today."

"You know where she is?" asks the man who answered my phone.

"Is that my eye inside on the phone?"

He nods. "She's in the attic. He saw Barone's widow and the man she claims to be her uncle coming out of a small door at the end of a hallway on the top floor." He listens for a moment, then adds, "The two of them were talking about how this is almost over, how they can finally be together, and how their facade of being relatives is about to be over for good."

None of their personal shit matters to me. Except for the fact that the Darius fucker is now on my list of who pays for taking my wife. And that's a list no motherfucker should want to be on. "Okay," I say as I look at the men in the room, "you guys know that asshole's head is on the chopping block."

"We'll be moving in soon," my guy tells my eye on the phone. "We'll go with the car bomb, so steer clear of the ground floor. Be available to show us where the package is located. We want to do this fast and without incident or injury."

With the call, we now know where my wife is, and the plan can be put into action. "Time to move. You all know what to do, and I expect this to go without a hitch. Operation Get Her Home is in effect."

As we all walk out of my office and head down the hallway, I spot my mother. Her eyes are full of worry, and as soon as I get to her, she asks, "What's going on?"

"I'm bringing her home." Kissing her on top of the head, I give her my best smile. "She'll be here in no time."

She clasps her hands together as if in prayer. "Thank you."

"Throw in a prayer for an easy operation while you're at it." I move on, wanting to get this thing going. "See you soon."

My driver pulls out, following a couple of other cars. Night has fallen, and that means no one will see us coming.

I call my inside guy back to hear for myself what he knows about my wife's whereabouts.

"Talk to me," I say.

"I'm on the top floor right now. There's a small door at the very top of a narrow set of stairs that I think lead to the attic."

"Can you get up there to make sure that's where my wife is?"

"I'll make it happen, boss."

My men talk among themselves, making plans, as I wait to see if he can get in.

I hear some rattling. "The door's locked," my inside eye says. "I have something that might get me in."

"We're on the way. You need to be able to get out of there fast once the shit hits the fan. Having her already with you when it's time to go would make me a happy man."

The car speeds around a sharp corner with no headlights on. Staying unseen is key. Brake lights ahead prompt my driver to slam on his brakes. "Fuck!" he shouts.

"Go around 'em!" one of my guys shouts. "Just floor it!"

"Damn. I can't get it to unlock," my inside guy tells me. "Hang on—I hear a knocking sound." He's quiet for a moment. "Isabella, are you in there?"

"Come on, baby. Let us know you're in there," I say as I stare into the darkness ahead.

"I hear something," he says. "It's muffled. It has to be her. I'm going to keep trying. I'll call you if I make it in and get her out."

"You'll hear it all go down in a few minutes." I end the call, looking around to make sure everything is as it should be.

"That's the alley behind their place," the driver calls out. "You guys ready?"

More than ready to get this thing done and over with, I give a nod. The men have the plan memorized and are ready to implement it. I take a deep breath as the car slows. Many of my men have already arrived, surrounded the house, and drawn their guns.

Chaos is key, and my guys are about to create a shit-ton of it. The bomb goes off, and flames shoot from the car, lighting up the darkness. Alarms go off as all hell breaks loose.

People pour out of the mansion, and at the same time, my men move into the opening created by the bomb. Part of the structure catches fire from the blaze, and I feel the need to speed things up.

Calling my man inside, I say, "Tell me you got her."

"I haven't gotten in yet. I can already smell the smoke though. I can tell we don't have much time." I hear rattling sounds and some cursing. "Fuck, these motherfuckers sure know how to make a lock."

People are running everywhere, and I know I need to go in. I can't sit here and depend on anyone else. "I'm going in," I let one of my men know just before I get out of the car.

He jumps out to follow me. "Boss, let me go instead!"

"You keep the motor running. I want to get the fuck out of here as soon as I have her." I turn to make sure he does as I say and watch as he gets back into the driver's seat. I can't let anything go wrong now. I have to get her out, and I need to do it yesterday.

I move through the mansion, staying close to the walls as I get my inside man back on the phone. "Where am I going?"

"Damn, you came in by yourself, huh? Didn't see that coming. Anyway, you came in the back, right? From where I heard the explosion?"

"Yes." Smoke fills the air, making it hard to breathe.

"Okay, there are stairs off that hallway. Come up them," he directs.

I can barely make out the stairs as the smoke is already getting thick. Once I find them, I go quickly and then ask, "I'm up. Now where?"

"To the right. Come all the way down." I can hear him coughing and know the smoke is thick where he is as well, and that means Isabella is probably being affected by it too.

I hear some muffled sounds on his end of the line. "Is that Isabella?"

"It sounds like it might be," he says.

"Tell her I'm almost there." I move fast, knowing there's little time left.

He coughs. "The smoke is getting really heavy up here."

"Rip off a piece of your shirt and hold it over your mouth to help filter the smoke." I can hardly see through the smoke in the darkness. "I'm at the end of this hall."

"Okay, there's a small door. Feel your way to it. The narrow staircase should be there if you're at the right place."

"Has she answered you yet?" I ask as I pull the door open and see the narrow steps he talked about.

"No. I don't think she can hear me. She's probably not in the room on the other side of this door but in a room beyond that. At least that's the way it sounds."

Making my way up the narrow staircase, I hear odd sounds coming from the wall. "What the hell is that?"

When I get to the top, I see my guy. "Sir, I hear shouting coming from inside. I think another woman is in there with her now too. But how she got there, I don't know."

"I heard something as I was coming up. Probably a passage through the top of a closet. I need to get this door open fast. You get the hell out of here."

"Are you sure you don't need my help?" he asks, his eyes darting back and forth.

"I've got this."

With a nod, he takes off, and I point my gun at the doorknob and fire, blowing the locking mechanism to oblivion. The sounds of the alarms going off all over the place mask the sound of the gun and me kicking in the door.

I can hear the murmur of voices, both male and female, coming from the other side of yet another door. The closer I get, the louder the voices get.

"Call off your dog!" I hear a woman say. I assume it's Vivian Barone.

"I don't know who you're talking about!" I hear Isabella shout. "Let me out of here, Vivian! This place is on fire. We're all going to die if we stay here."

A man shouts, "You're not getting out of here!"

The fuck she's not.

"Just unlock the fucking door," Isabella shouts.

Then I hear lots of footsteps, and it sounds to me like they might be scuffling.

"Stop!" the man screams. "Just stop!"

"Stop! I'm not letting you out, Isabella," Vivian shouts. "Use my phone to call your husband and tell him to stop this right now."

"Your fucking house is on fire, you stupid bitch!" Isabella cries out. "He can't stop what's already happened. We need to get the fuck out of here. I don't want to burn alive. Do you?"

"She's right," the man says. "We have to leave. Come on."

"If we leave, she'll get out," the woman says. "I can't let her get away."

"We will all die!" Isabella says.

I kick the door, and it won't budge. No one seems to hear it from the inside.

If I take a shot at the doorknob, the bullet might end up going through and hitting my wife. I can't take that chance. But I know it'll take me a while to kick the door in.

Leaning against the wall, I close my eyes and try not to choke on the thick smoke. I have to get to my wife. That's all that matters.

I try to take a breath, but nothing happens. I've inhaled too much smoke.

I don't have time for this shit!

Chapter 20

Isabella

What's that?

Three knocks on the door make me step way back, feeling the need to take cover. I have no idea what's on the other side of the door, but it sounds like it's about to burst through.

Darius is trying to drag Vivian back to the trap door they came through, but she's fighting him. Then something erupts—a blast of orange and yellow sparks and a sound so loud my hands instinctively cover my ears. I duck down by the side of the bed.

A shriek fills the air, and I look up to see Vivian falling backward. "What the fuck?" Darius shouts.

Another burst of sparks, and he's thrown backward. And then I see something I thought I would never see again. "Carlo!"

He looks at the bodies on the floor and then at the chains holding me to the bed. "Where is the key?"

"Vivian!" I shout and point to her prone body. I knew he would come for me, but I still can't believe he's here. The man himself, the boss, came for me. I always had hope that he would be the one to come through that door.

As soon as he retrieves the keys, he moves fast to get to me and unlocks the padlock. I can't stop touching his face, wanting to make sure he's real. "You're here."

His mouth crashes against mine, and I wrap my arms around him, not wanting to let go. But we have more important things to deal with than showing how much we've missed each other.

He pulls his mouth away from mine, and I can't stop looking at him, can't stop wondering if this is real. He holds me tightly for a moment and then turns to lead me out of my prison. "Let's get the hell out of here!"

"I'm ready, babe!"

We move as fast as we can through the heavy smoke, but it fills my lungs, and I can't stop coughing. Carlo stops, tears off a piece of his shirt, and hands it to me. I cover my mouth with it, and we keep moving.

We walk down a long hallway and run into two disheveled young women. They look at us with frightened eyes and ask, "Have you seen our mother?"

"Vivian?" I ask.

They nod, and then Carlo says, "Come with us."

I look at him with confusion for a brief moment. I can't help wondering what he plans to do with them. They're young, and none of this is their fault.

Carlo leads all of us through the burning mansion. The heat is nearly overwhelming as we get to the bottom floor, and everything seems to be on fire.

A crashing sound comes from beside us, and I reach out to grab Vivian's girls, pulling them to me, instinctively wanting to protect them. An entire flaming wall falls down to the side of us, and a plume of water follows it. The water forms a small stream when it lands on the floor.

Carlo leads us out of the inferno. People are everywhere, and they all cheer as we walk out of what seems like an impossible situation.

Carlo scoops me into his arms and carries me to the waiting car. Resting my head against my hero's chest, I begin to cry. "It's over. It's finally over."

He presses his lips against the top of my head. "You can't do this to me again."

"I'll try not to." When I hug him, I can feel the love coming from him.

Before I know it, we're all in the car, speeding away from the fiery scene. Vivian's girls sit across from us in the limo, looking like little scared rabbits. "Um, do you know where our mom is?" one of them asks.

I shake my head and look at them with sympathy. "I'm sorry."

Carlo asks, "You girls have anything to do with kidnapping this woman?"

I grasp his hand and give it a squeeze. "Please, they've been through hell. My father was horrible to them."

He looks past me at the girls. "Answer me."

"No, sir," says one of them. "We aren't told much of anything. Our mother and father said we were to be seen but not heard. We stay in our bedrooms mostly."

"If I ever find out anything different, I will deal with you both. You get me?" Carlo's voice, strict and threatening, makes me worry that he would hurt the young teens.

"I'm sure they're telling the truth," I tell him, trying to calm him down a little. "I never saw them or heard anything about them being involved in any way. What I did hear from their mother is how badly my father treated them. They're my half sisters." I look into his eyes and ask, "Can we take care of them? They have no one now."

"If everything comes back clean on them, we'll take care of them like they're family. If not . . ." He doesn't have to say anything else.

The girls and I know well what his silence means. Although I want the poor girls' horror story to end with the death of their parents, I know I can't ask my husband to blindly take them in. I know he's doing what's best for the family.

"Thank you."

"Don't thank me yet," he warns me and them at the same time. But he smiles slightly, and I take that as a good sign. My husband is a good man. He may be a Mafia king, but he's a good man, and I'm proud to call him mine.

I begin the introductions. "So, I'm Isabella, your big sister. And this is my husband, Carlo. And your names are?"

"I'm Lisa," the older one says. She looks at Carlo. "Thank you for saving us and not leaving us back there. I don't know much about things, but I know loyalty means a lot to people like us. So, I pledge my loyalty to you, sir."

"Me too," the younger girl says. "I'm Mary, and I want to say thank you for saving us too. I will always be loyal to you, sir. I promise." She looks at me. "You're really our sister that we've heard about? Your mom stole you from our father. My mom said it was what she did that made our father as mean as he was."

Shaking my head, I say, "From what I have heard about our father, he was a very mean man before my mother left and took me away. I'm sorry for all the bad things you must have been through. As long as my husband allows it, I will make your lives much better than they have been."

With a nod, Carlo says, "As long as you two devote yourselves to me and your sister, we're good."

"No problem there," Lisa is quick to say. "I had nothing to do with any of this mess. I'm the quiet one. That's served me well all these years."

The girls hug each other and then look at me. "Thank you both so much," they say at the same time.

I smile at them. "Hey, we're happy to have you."

"We're happy to have you too," Mary says. "I'm ready to move on to something better. Life so far has been kind of sucky."

"Way sucky," Lisa agrees.

Later that night, we lie in our bed together. I can't stop crying as I realize how close we came to losing each other. "I'm sorry for letting them take me out of that store."

"They drugged you." He kisses my lips softly. "If you'd had the ability to get away from them, I'm sure you would've. And if your guards had stayed close enough to you, it wouldn't have happened at all."

I can only imagine what happened to the men who were guarding me that day. But that's not what I want to think about right now.

"I'm just so glad to be here, home, in our bed together." I know he would walk through fire for me, and there's no one else in this entire world who could ever love me more than he does.

His lips press against mine, taking me to the depths of the abyss only he can take me to. Drowning in our love is the best feeling ever. But I've got something to tell my husband that might make him very happy.

When he eases his kiss, I whisper, "I think I'm pregnant."

He emits a low growl before turning into a straight-up savage, claiming me in every way imaginable. I could not be happier to belong to this man!

***

Carlo

Eight months later...

I can't seem to take my eyes off the sight of my wife as she feeds our baby from her plump breast. "A boy. You gave me a boy.

I swore all the way until I saw his little pecker that you were having a girl."

"I kept telling you that I felt like it was a boy." Running her finger over his little forehead, she sighs. "He looks like you."

"He's got my hair, but his nose is yours." Kissing the top of her head, I wonder if I could ever have more love in my heart than I do at this moment. "We have a son. Our firstborn. But all I had picked out was a girl's name. We have to figure out what we're naming our son."

Looking at me with shining eyes, she asks, "Is there anyone you have in mind right now?"

I have the feeling she's the one with someone in mind. "You tell me first."

"He's no longer with us. He was a real hero, just like you. I miss him every single day, and I know you do too." A tear falls, and she swipes it away before it can fall on the baby.

I know who she's talking about. "He never had any children of his own. It wasn't a thing we ever talked about. But I bet he would have made a great father to some lucky kid."

"He was a good big brother to me." Wiping away another tear, she sniffles. "Then we agree?"

Nodding, I ask, "What about a middle name?"

Staring at our son, she grins and then looks at me. "What if we name him after you too? Not a junior, but still your name. Or a form of it."

Nodding, I like the way it sounds, even if it's just in my mind. "I like it. You know my mother's going to call him something silly though, right?"

"Of course. She's so excited right now that she's probably sitting in the nursery waiting for us to come home so she can take him over."

The door to the hospital room flies open, and her sisters, Lisa and Mary, come inside. "He's here!"

The girls have stayed loyal and stood by their words. It's obvious that life under the rule of Daniel Barone was cruel. His daughters have all suffered because of him. But I won't let them suffer any further.

"We got the place down the street from you guys after all," Lisa says.

Isabella's overjoyed expression says it all. "I'm so happy you two are going to be living so close to us! I loved that mansion the first time I laid eyes on it. You girls are going to be so happy there. I just know it."

"You made it happen, big sis," Mary tells her as she takes a seat on the hospital bed, then runs her hand over her little nephew's head. "Lisa and I went to the bank and opened a savings account for our new nephew with some of the money you gave us, Isabella. We want to make sure he knows his aunties only want the best for him, the way you two have made sure you only want what's best for us."

"Hey, it's your money. You can do with it whatever you want. You both paid dearly your entire lives. You deserve something in return for the drama and pain you had to go through. Anyway, my husband provides for me and our family very well. He wanted you girls to have enough to live on for the rest of your lives. He's a generous man." My wife's eyes sparkle as she gazes at me.

With my blessing, Isabella gave a sizeable amount of the money and physical property of the estate that she inherited from her father to the girls. Then, I distributed his organization's employees and the rest of his assets among my family members' organizations right here in the New York area. My cousins and I will now truly be the kings of the New York underworld.

I felt it best to dissolve the Barone family once and for all. When power is used to abuse the women and children, then it must be diffused. None of Barone's men were strong enough to keep the family. I suppose they'd had their share of Daniel's punishments, and it made them want to move on and leave the family in the past.

Once upon a time in Palermo, Italy, two men fell in love with the same woman and began a decades-long war that their grandchildren ended by getting married and starting a family in New York, New York, America.

They say love conquers all. Maybe that's true. Maybe love is the strongest thing of all.

"Allow me to introduce you to the firstborn of the Vietti family," my wife says as she holds up our son. "John Carlito Vietti will take over his father's throne one day to become the king of New York."

Mary and Lisa laugh and bow. "All hail, King John Carlito!"

All I can think about is what a great Mafia king name that is. My wife isn't wrong. He will take over where I leave off. I just hope I raise him to be the best Mafia king there has ever been or ever will be.

But my real hope for him is that he finds a Mafia queen to love as much as I love his mother. We all deserve a happy ending, and we've found ours.

The End

Thank you for reading Deadly Don's Arranged Vows.

If you loved this book, then you'll love **Deadly Don's Secret Baby**!

It's a fast paced enemies to lovers Mafia romance that's bound to steam up your reading glasses.

(To get Deadly Don's Secret Baby visit: htttps://www.amazon.com/dp/B0CTQYDCT1)

After declaring war on organized crime the daughter of a newly elected mayor is kidnapped and held for ransom by a New York Mafia Don. An unexpected love story then follows resulting in two pink lines and a sweet HEA ending. Read chapter one on the very next page!

Deadly Don's Secret Baby Sneak Peek

Introduction

I've been kidnapped by a Mafia grump who's given me a secret baby bump.

My father is the newly elected mayor and is at war with my captor.

Giovanni, a casino billionaire, is chiseled out of marble and simply irresistible. The perfect specimen of an alpha man with one problem - his heart is stone like the rest of him.

While locked in chains I'm seduced and thrust into seventh heaven. I never knew sinning with the enemy could feel this good.

Now with a baby growing inside me and my father refusing to negotiate, I dread that my unborn child will become the new bargaining chip.

With each passing day, the tension between us rises… As the man of stone has to choose between his criminal empire or his future heir.

(To get Deadly Don's Secret Baby visit: https://www.amazon.com/dp/B0CTQYDCT1)

Chapter One

Giovanni

Who the fuck does this guy think he is?

My right eye twitches, my nerves already on edge, and the man's only served one damn day as mayor of the city I run. "You know, maybe he don't know how things work here in Mount Vernon."

"Maybe he needs to be told, Boss." Larry the Snake is one of my best men. If anyone can make this asshole mayor see the light, it'd be him.

"You might wanna visit this moron." Tossing back a shot of vodka, I pray it takes the edge off so my goddamn eye will stop twitching.

"Maybe you should nip this problem in the bud, Son." My father holds up a bottle of red wine as he comes into the office on the top floor of my casino. "I won this on one of the nickel slots. Just my luck, huh?"

"How do you think I should handle this?" My old man knows more about handling business than anyone I know in my organization. I trust every word that comes out of his mouth.

"Let me hear what the man has to say." He takes the remote for the television then rewinds it so he can see what we're talking about.

"Congratulations, Mayor Ricci, on your landslide victory," the reporter says with a smile. "As everyone knows, you are the high school principal of one of Mount Vernon's highest ranked schools in the New York area. Would you care to tell our viewers how you're going to leave your mark on our fair city?"

"Glad to," the smarmy old man says with a shit-eating grin. "See, I've got ideas that will change everything. We don't want to be like all the New York boroughs, full of criminal activity. That's why way back in 1894, when the citizens of Mount Vernon got to vote about becoming a New York borough or becoming an independent municipality, they chose the latter. We are our own city and want nothing like the lives of those who call New York their home. We want to be better than that. We want to know we're safe when we walk the sidewalks, drive the streets, and do business. If we're going to get back to the way things were before organized crime began creeping into our city, then we're going to have to go to war with the crime bosses who brought their illegal businesses here in the first place. I'm here to stomp out organized crime in Mount Vernon, New York, just the way I promised you all that I would when I ran for mayor."

My father pauses the television and looks at me with fire in his eyes. "You have to stop this guy or he's gonna make life pretty fucking miserable for a whole lotta people."

"Any ideas how I should go about it, Pop?"

"You see them broads standing behind him?"

Looking closer, I see what looks like the man's wife and the other is probably his daughter. "Pretty good-looking broads."

"Yeah, they are," Pop agrees. "Use the girl to get to him."

"Take his daughter hostage." With a nod, I know what I have to do. "She's gonna be some fun to play with, I can tell you that much." It's been a while since I got to torture a young beauty like her anyway. About time I had some fun in my life again.

Watching the television screen, some things begin to pop out at me. The young woman I believe to be the mayor's daughter has long, dark hair tucked neatly behind each ear. Her blue eyes sparkle brilliantly, and her ruby red lips are plump and utterly kissable. Her body is round in all the right places too.

Then there's the woman who stands next to her. A broad-shouldered woman, she stands a foot taller than her adult daughter. Thin, wispy, pale blonde hair cut short like a boys is nothing like her daughter's thick mane. There is nothing about them that's even similar.

"You notice how the mom and daughter don't look alike?" Pointing at the television screen, I find the father doesn't resemble his daughter either. "And look at the mayor. He's fat. Even with that expensive suit on, you can still tell he's fat. And his hair is gray, but you can still see a tiny bit of red hair at his temples. The girl is gorgeous, her mother is on the hideous side, and her father is about as ugly as they come."

My father shrugs. "With the way girls gussy themselves up, there's no telling what she's done to make her appear much different than she really looks."

"Well, she couldn't have made herself shorter." Laughing, I think about how I'll soon have the young woman in my clutches and then I'll find out what is fake on her and what's real. "I look forward to having her as my captive."

My father's eyes glisten as he fills a glass with the wine he won. "See, if you had yourself a real woman to call your own, you wouldn't get so excited about the one you're about to kidnap. You're not getting any younger, Giovanni."

"I'm forty-two, not quite an old man as you would have me think I am. And I don't want to marry just anyone, Pop. You should know that better than anyone. I am to marry to keep our bloodline pure."

"I'm glad you've remembered that, Son. I didn't marry for love. I married for power and blood. It has served me well. My wife, your saint of a mother, has been the rock I never knew I needed. And your wife, if chosen well, will be the same for you."

"I haven't found the right woman with all the criteria I insist on. And you haven't found one for me either. In the meantime, I can play with anyone I wish. And I might wish to play with my soon-to-be hostage. Sending her back home with any dignity is not an option."

"Of course, it's not." Sipping the wine, my father makes a dreadful face. "This is no better than horse piss!"

"Why would I give away good wine at my casino?" I'm no fool. "I didn't get where I am today by giving away good things. If you want the good stuff, you have to pay for it."

"You are a financial genius." Dad leaves the glass and bottle on the table before taking out his cell phone. "We got to get this plan in motion before someone else grabs that broad. I'm calling in my brothers to help make the plan. You better get us something to eat. You know those bastards get cranky when there's no food around to keep them happy."

"A whole meal or some finger foods?" Larry asks as he puts himself in charge of the meal planning.

"It's going to be a long night of planning. So what do you think, Snake?" Dad's frown says it all. When Italians get together for pretty much any occasion, lots of food needs to be available to them and lots of wine too. The good kind.

I pause the news report, focusing on the woman who I will have in my home very soon. There's a strength that shows in her eyes. It'll be my pleasure to drain her of any and all strength she has. When she's returned to her moron of a father, he won't find the woman he saw last. He'll find a shell of a woman, almost unrecognizable as his daughter. And he will never again attempt to cross anyone in the business we're in.

For centuries politicians and law men all over the world have made vain attempts at stopping the kinds of business me and my ancestors have built. For reasons I cannot figure out, the idiots still try to end something they don't understand at all.

"Cannoli?" Larry looks at me for the answer.

"Of course, cannoli." Shaking my head, I don't know why he even had to ask. "That's like asking if you should order meatballs."

"Yeah, you're right, Boss. I'm thinking about a cheesecake too."

My mind isn't on food at the moment, so I merely nod. There's a lot to think about. The kidnapping of a family member of a public figure will mean vast amounts of publicity. And that will mean that we will have to watch our backs.

Fortunately, our organization has ties to families in New York. The mayor and the authorities won't be able to pin-point the exact family to charge with the kidnapping. Which makes things a bit easier for us.

"When the others get here, we'll get right to work." Pop settles into his favorite chair. "When will these fuckers stop trying to end something that's bigger than they can even imagine? It's like they can't wrap their tiny heads around the fact that we've always been here, and we always will be. Whether anyone likes it or not."

Yeah, we're not going anywhere!

(To get Deadly Don's Secret Baby visit: https://www.amazon.com/dp/B0CTQYDCT1)

Printed in Great Britain
by Amazon